Murder by Boojum

Murder by Boojum

A Mystery in Eight Fits
inspired by Lewis Carroll's
The Hunting of the Snark

by Byron W. Sewell

Illustrated by
The Author

evertype
2014

Published by Evertype, Cnoc Sceichín, Leac an Anfa, Cathair na Mart, Co. Mhaigh Eo, Éire. *www.evertype.com*.

A catalogue record for this book is available from the British Library.

ISBN-10 1-78201-079-3
ISBN-13 978-1-78201-079-1

Typeset in De Vinne Text, Mona Lisa, ENGRAVERS' ROMAN, and *Liberty* by Michael Everson.

Illustrations: Byron W. Sewell.

Cover: Michael Everson.

Printed by LightningSource.

Foreword

SNARK CLUBS

There are at least two genuine snark clubs. Perhaps the oldest, and certainly the most famous, is The Snark Club, founded in 1934 at the University of Cambridge. However, that society is not (at least now, anyway) a secret society and has become quite public in their activities, inviting the public to apply to attend one of their annual meetings, though how often such an invitation is extended is unknown to me. They even have a website (www.snark.com) in case you might like to apply. They recently posted a group photograph of those in attendance at the 2013 annual meeting. One person of note in the photograph is Dr Selwyn H. Goodacre (first row on the left-hand corner), the world's foremost textual authority on the *Alice* books and author or editor of many articles and books about Charles Dodgson and his works, including *The Hunting of the Snark*.[1]

The other functioning English snark club (The Universal Snark Club; TUSC) attempts to remain more-or-less secret, but in spite of their vows of secrecy some of their activities

---

1 The publisher quite naturally recommends the Evertype edition, published in 2010 (ISBN 978-1-904808-36-7

have become known (or at least rumored). The TUSC meets annually at Christ Church in Oxford.

Both of these English clubs have only ten members at any given time; each assigned a name of one of the crewmen from the poem. Their chairman (Captain, in this sense) is designated "The Bellman". At each meeting someone (or perhaps more than one) typically makes (or procures) in a very limited number something related to snarks (usually of an original or creative nature) to be distributed to those in attendance as a keepsake or memento. These are understandably rare, since they were produced in very limited editions and usually enter the private Carroll collections of most of those in attendance. They are prized collector's items, only rarely (if ever) appearing on the market. For example, I have never seen one of these keepsakes offered on eBay, though this doesn't necessarily mean that they have never appeared. One particularly clever and funny item by the late Alan White, *Report of an Investigation / into Bellman Enterprises' Snark Safari*, written for the TUSC's 1996 meeting, was published in 2011 for members of The Lewis Carroll Society and The Lewis Carroll Society of North America.

Unlike the Cambridge Snark Club, the Oxford club is not open to the public and those in attendance are by invitation only, though some members are known to be accompanied by their spouses, so there will typically be more than ten people in attendance.

At one time there was a West Coast Chapter of The Lewis Carroll Society of North America (LCSNA), founded by Dr Sandor G. Burstein, a prominent Carroll collector. However, as far as I know, there was never an organized snark club associated with the West Coast Chapter. The snark society described in this book is fictitious. Further, there is no actual American Lewis Carroll Society.

Unlike the infamous Victorian-era "Cannibal Club" founded by Sir Richard Burton (see Wikipedia for a brief description), there has never been so much as a hint of anything outrageous, deviant or criminal happening during a meeting of a snark club. That may be disappointing to some of you. Hopefully, this present violent tale will make up for that unfortunate fact

For those of you who are interested in such things, an earlier unillustrated version of this tale was originally published privately in a very limited edition for private distribution in 2000 as one of three stories in what I refer to as my "Millennium Snark Trilogy", under the title "SNARK! A Murderous Agony in Eight Fits". This present publication is the third in the trilogy, the other two ("Snarkmaster"[2] and "Atchafalaya Boojum"[3]) having already been published by Evertype.

Byron Sewell
Hurricane, 2014

---

2 *Snarkmaster: A Destiny in Eight Fits* (ISBN 978-1-78201-002-9)
3 *In the Boojum Forest* (ISBN 978-1-78201-078-4)

CONTENTS

Fit I

Forks

Forks

The heavy padded mailer looked innocent enough to Fred Poole. It had a picture of a trout on the lower left-hand corner and the return label was for the California Department of Fish and Game. Even though he hadn't ordered anything from them, he assumed that it contained a book and went ahead and opened it without phoning them to verify that they had actually sent him one. It was the biggest mistake of his life. The full force of the bomb struck him in the chest, tore off two fingers, blinded an eye, and ruptured an eardrum.

The explosion was loud enough for the receptionist in the insurance agency next door to his own office to place a 911 call. Sirens screamed, shrill and high, rending the shuddering sky as the police, rescue squad and a fire truck arrived. He was still alive when the EMTs found him. Since it was apparent that there had been a bomb explosion they got him out of the building as quickly as possible and set to work, trying to keep him alive until they could get him to a hospital. Firemen did a quick search of his office and found his missing fingers, which they rushed down to the ambulance, where they were packed in ice in hopes that it might be possible to reattach them.

Police quickly organized an evacuation of the building in case there was a second bomb, herding the occupants leaving the building a block down the street as a precaution. Since it was almost lunchtime, most of the evacuees went into the Three Oceans Chinese restaurant, which was close to the staging point, and enjoyed their blistering Szechwan buffet while awaiting the all-clear signal. Bomb specialists donned full body armour and used sniffing dogs to thoroughly search the building. Having assured themselves that there were no additional explosive devices in the building, they allowed its occupants to return to their offices several hours later. Six ATF and FBI agents in dark suits soon arrived from Los Angeles.

Bombings were rare in Fresno and the FPD, who had local jurisdiction, didn't have investigators who specialized in them. So the case was assigned to Homicide Detectives Brad Pinkman and Jesse Jinks. They had been partners for eight years and neither one of them had ever had occasion to personally witness the aftereffects of a bombing. But even if they had seen them on a regular basis they would have found this one unique. Whoever had built the bomb had packed it with pieces of silverware to create shrapnel; forks to be exact. The hospital report, a copy of which the ATF Agency had condescended to send them the next morning, indicated that surgeons had removed three tines from Mr. Poole's chest. This shrapnel had punctured both lungs, miraculously missing his heart, and he had almost bled to death before they could repair the damage, which had involved the removal of one lobe. He was listed in stable but critical condition, and was expected to survive.

It was another two days before the ATF and FBI shared a copy of the crime lab report with the FPD. A number of fork fragments had been dug out of the walls and ceiling of the office, along with the pieces that had even been extracted from Poole's chest and from a stuffed bull elk head that hung over his desk. Photos of the fork fragments were attached to the report, clearly showing where the fork handles had been sawn off and discarded. They had been identified as being from patterns sold at Sears, Penny's and Montgomery Wards in the 1940s.

"There's no way they're ever going to trace those," Jinks remarked.

"I expect you're right," agreed Pinkman. "The bomber could have bought them at any of thousands of flea markets or antique shops."

The ATF report also identified the explosive as Semtex, the explosive of choice for many of the world's terrorists, primarily because they could manufacture it themselves, using the instructions in a little red booklet that had been readily available at gun shows until it had been outlawed. However, the most interesting thing in the report was that there had been a message placed in the bomb, carefully engraved onto a small strip of stainless steel designed to survive the blast. It read: "They pursued it with forks and hope". The ATF had identified this as a quote from *The Hunting of the Snark*, a rather obscure Lewis Carroll nonsense poem. Pinkman remembered it from an English course he had taken in junior college. "What I tell you three times is true," he thought; it was the only other line from the poem that he could recall.

The bomb had been mailed from Chowchilla, north of Fresno, and the FBI had already interviewed the post office there, finding that no one could remember it. That was all that was in the report. Other than the quote from the poem, there wasn't much to go on.

"I wonder if there's a Lewis Carroll society." Pinkman asked.

"I wouldn't be surprised," said Jinks. "These days there's a society for just about everything, from beer cans to license plates. We could check the internet," he suggested.

Pinkman quickly found the home page for the American Lewis Carroll Society, an elaborate site with over a hundred pages, filled with sophisticated graphics, Dodgson photographs, texts, and chitchat about Carroll in the popular culture. When he e-mailed the Society's secretary, Alicia Wunderlich, he found that the FBI had already contacted her as well, something that they had failed to mention in their report. Mrs. Wunderlich e-mailed him a copy of the same membership list that she had given to the FBI. He printed it out, then emailed the English Society, requesting a copy of their membership list as well. The English Society's secretary responded that she had no intention of releasing their membership list to someone she didn't know without instruction from the Foreign Office, and told him to make any such requests through the British Consulate. He decided to drop that idea for the time being. "Can you believe this?" he said. "There are Carroll societies in Canada, Brazil, The Netherlands, Italy, Germany, Japan, Australia, Iceland, Nigeria, and even Papua New Guinea!"

"Papua New Guinea?"

"That's what's listed. There are 2,500 names on this list for the American Lewis Carroll Society! Thankfully two dozen of them are listed as deceased, so that helps a little, I suppose." He did a quick count. "There are forty members who are universities and other such institutions. If we eliminate all of those it still leaves about twenty-four hundred. I wouldn't have thought that Carroll was *that* popular."

"Who'd a thought? Tracking down that lot should keep the FBI busy for a while! Talk about dog work!"

"Half of them are probably school kids and little old ladies."

"That'd be my guess," replied Jinks. "Let me see the list." He studied it for a few minutes then said, "I vote we concentrate on members with California addresses, especially members of their California Chapter. Look! Here's our victim." Jinks held up the list, pointing to a name. "Fred Poole's a member of both the American Lewis Carroll Society and their California Chapter."

"You have to wonder why a taxidermist like Poole would be interested in Lewis Carroll."

"You have to wonder why any adult is," responded the Jinks. "If you ask me, these people are all stuck in their childhood."

"Like you and basketball?" Pinkman responded.

"Low blow! That's different," Jinks protested.

"Yeah, right! Let's give the California Chapter's president a call and see what he can tell us." Pinkman dialled his listed work phone number, and Jinks got on an extension.

A woman with an Australian accent answered. "Doctor Kerr's office. May I help you?"

Pinkman identified himself, then asked to speak with Dr. Kerr. "I'm sorry, but he's with a patient. Can he call you back in about ten minutes?"

"That'll be fine." He gave her the number.

About fifteen minutes later Dr. Kerr was on the line. Pinkman introduced himself. "We're investigating a bombing that happened here in Fresno. You may have heard or read about it."

"Indeed. It's been big news in the L. A. papers and on local TV."

"Were you aware that the victim, Mr. Fred Poole, is a member of your California Chapter of the American Lewis Carroll Society?"

"Yes. I recognized his name. The Chapter sent flowers. I've met him on several occasions, at various Chapter meetings. I don't know him well, though."

"Can you think of any reason why anyone would want to harm him?"

"As I told the FBI, I haven't any idea whatsoever. You have to understand that we are a literary society. With rare exception, we don't get to know each other on a very intimate basis. We correspond occasionally and sometimes see each other at meetings; that's usually about it. No one would ever talk about his or her enemies."

"Are you aware that the bomb included a quote from a Lewis Carroll poem?"

"Yes, I read that in the papers; a line from *The Hunting of the Snark*."

"Is there anyone in the Society who has a special interest in this particular poem?"

"Of course. Many of us do. Almost any Carroll collector would have copies of the book. However, there is a much greater interest in *Alice*, of course."

"Do any of your members have an exceptionally large collection of Snark editions?"

"Well, I have about three hundred copies."

"Really?" Pinkman asked, amazed at what he had heard. "Yes." He paused. "I hope that doesn't mean I'm a suspect!"

"I didn't mean to imply that. I'm curious; why do you have so many?"

"My wife has asked me the same thing on numerous occasions. I don't know, really; I just like them. Can't get enough of a good thing, I suppose."

"Are there other collectors who would have that many editions?"

"I doubt it. But I can think of at least a dozen collectors who would have twenty or thirty copies: there are several in New York, one in Maryland, two in Massachusetts, one in Illinois, half a dozen or more here in California ... "

"Can you give me the names of the California ones?" Pinkman interrupted him.

"Well, there's me, as I said earlier. Then there's Cooksley, Schwartz, Barnett, Clapham, Imhoff, Cleaver, and, oh yes, Fred Poole; your victim."

"Fred Poole?"

"Yes, I think so. I've never had the opportunity to see his entire collection, but I know that he has some rare things associated with *The Snark*, so I would definitely say he had a more than casual interest in it."

"What kind of special things does he have?" Pinkman asked.

"Well, he has a couple of presentation copies from Dodgson to some child-friends, one of which is a rare purple binding variant. And he has some original art from Mahendra Singh's edition of *The Snark*. Things of that nature. "

"Did Poole have any enemies in the Society?"

"Not that I know of. In fact, I don't know of anyone in the Society that has enemies. Our members are pretty nice people: academicians, housewives, school children, artists, and collectors; that sort of thing. Our meetings are all very genial and fun. If anyone has enemies they don't talk about them at our functions."

Pinkman thanked him and rang off.

"That group sounds about as boring as watching a curling match," Jinks said.

"You don't like curling?"

"Well, to tell the truth I've never seen a match; just a few clips on TV. It's always some squatting woman with her mouth wide open, yelling like someone just dropped her stone on her big toe. So now what?"

"Let's go pay Fred Poole's wife a visit; see if she has any ideas."

"The FBI would have been there already."

"I know; they seem to be omnipresent. But they aren't going to share much with us; and perhaps they haven't yet followed the *Snark* trail."

"Before we go let's check with ATF and find out if there are any open cases with Lewis Carroll associations," Jinks suggested.

"That's a good idea. Our bomber may be interested in *Alice* as well as *Snarks*."

Jinks placed the call and took a few notes. "They had already checked this angle. There isn't much to go on here. There was a theft of a first edition of *Alice* from a rare book room at the University of Illinois at Urbana-Champaign back in 1953; it's never been recovered. In 1956 there was an armed robbery in Sistersville, West Virginia in which some guy in a ski mask stole a can of film for a 1933 *Alice in Wonderland* movie at gunpoint. In 1967 some guy was shot dead in his Memphis living room while reading *Through the Looking-Glass*. That's all they came up with. There haven't been any previous bombings associated with anything Carrollian."

"Perhaps this bombing has more to do with Poole being a taxidermist than with Carroll," Pinkman suggested.

"How's that?"

"Oh, 1 don't know. Perhaps some environmental nut doesn't like him because he's associated with hunting elk. He has that big one on the wall behind his desk."

"I kind of doubt it; the bomber didn't include a quote from some famous tree-hugger."

"True." Pinkman turned and checked his e-mail again. "Listen to this! Ms. Wunderlich sent me another e-mail. She says that one of their former members wrote a parody of *Alice in Wonderland* back in 1974, entitled *R. A. V. E. N., or The Dormouse Who Came in from the Cold*. It's about a republican plot to overthrow the Queen of Hearts, by assassinating her with a homemade bomb made out of an explosive mixture of pepper and treacle. She thought we ought to check this guy out, since he seemed to be fascinated with bombs."

Jesse groaned. "This case is going to be really weird."

"And you said their Society was boring!"

Just as they got up to walk out to their car Detective Cox handed Pinkman a copy of the local newspaper. "Thought you guys might enjoy today's edition," he said. "The headline blared POLICE HUNTING FOR SNARKS. You guys watch out now," Cox told them with a big grin. "You bump into a BOOOO-jum Snark and you just might vanish!"

Everyone in the squad room had been listening and they all laughed. Then Cox suddenly yelled, "BOO!" at the top of his voice, which caused Pinkman to instinctively jerk his hand up to his pistol grip. This made everyone laugh even louder. "You better go take a Valium, Brad," Cox said.

"Very funny," Pinkman responded. He and Jinks walked on out to get in their car. Pinkman kept the newspaper.

"Let's drop by and visit Ms. Cookesly before we go over to Poole's place. Her house is on the way."

They drove there and got out. Pinkman knocked on the front door and an attractive, conservatively dressed woman opened it. He showed her his ID badge, then introduced himself and his partner. She invited them in.

"We're investigating the Fred Poole bombing," Pinkman told her. "Did you know him?"

"Quite well," she said. "It's so tragic. I do hope he will recover."

"I believe that's the prognosis. How did you know him?"

"Through a Carroll society we both belong to."

"The American Lewis Carroll Society?"

"Yes. How did you know?"

"If you've read today's newspaper, you know there was a quote from *The Hunting of the Snark* in the bomb."

"Yes, I read that. Very strange! I kept the paper actually; for my collection."

"You have a collection about bombings?"

"No, no! I kept it for my Lewis Carroll collection."

"Oh; I misunderstood you." He chuckled.

"Actually, I keep everything I find that has anything to do with him. Most Carroll collectors I know find it impossible to throw anything away that has even the slightest reference to Lewis Carroll."

"That reminds me of the bumper sticker about toys," Pinkman said. "I can imagine one that says: THE ONE WITH THE MOST CARROLL STUFF WHEN HE DIES WINS THE GAME."

She laughed. "Yes. That's a good idea. I think I'll see if I can get the California Chapter to have some printed up."

"Well, because of the reference to *The Snark* that was found in the bomb debris we obtained a list of members of the various Carroll societies here in America and your name came up."

"Why would my name come up?" suddenly alarmed that she might be a suspect.

"Dr. Kerr said that you shared a special interest in *The Hunting of the Snark* with Fred Poole."

"Oh, I see. Yes, that's correct; as I said, I'm a rather omnivorous collector. I have a relatively large number of editions of *The Snark*, as does Fred."

"Can you think of anyone who would have wanted to kill him?"

"No one; he's a very nice person."

"I wonder if we could ask you a favour? Would you mind showing us a few *Snarks* from your collection; just to educate us a bit? It's not something you find on the shelf of your local Barnes & Noble."

"No, it isn't. I'd be delighted to show you what I have. I keep my Carroll collection in my bedroom." She stood up and led them through the house. Her collection was prominently displayed in bookcases on a wall next to a large Victorian brass bed, covered by a frilly lace spread. The walls were lined with framed posters from various Disney productions of *Alice in*

Wonderland, some in foreign languages. Pinkman could recognize Japanese, Hangul, Hindi, and Russian.

"How many books do you have?" Pinkman asked, looking at the full shelves.

"I'm not sure. I've never counted them. There's probably something like a few thousand items in my collection, though they're not all books. There might be a thousand books I suppose."

"I assume these would be quite valuable," he said.

"Well, yes. I have the collection insured for two-hundred-thousand dollars. But, the way prices keep going up on this material that likely wouldn't replace it if something happened to it, God forbid! I can only rarely afford to buy anything to add to my collection these days. Books I used to buy for $20 or $30 now fetch $250 to $500."

Pinkman whistled. "So this is an investment?"

"Sort of, I suppose; though I wouldn't sell it for anything." She went over to a shelf and pulled down a couple of books. She handed a tan book to Pinkman and a large black one to Jinks. "This is the standard 1876 first edition," she said to Pinkman. "The one I gave you, Detective Jinks, is a strange 1974 production, published by the Catalpa Press in London. Here let me show you." She took the book back and walked across the large bedroom, and laid the book on the floor. She then proceeded to pull the folded pages out to a length of about fifteen feet. "This is called concertina style," she explained. "The Victorians used to make books that way. This crazy long boat in the illustration is the first chapter, or 'Fit' as Carroll called it, and depicts all of the ten crewmen who went hunting for Snarks. The illustrations are rather naively adapted after the original ones by Henry Holiday. Here, you can see the originals in the first edition you are holding, Detective Pinkman." They looked at a few.

"Have there been lots of different editions?" Jinks asked.

"Not lots; nothing like the *Alice* books, which probably runs into the thousands. A new edition of *The Snark* comes out every five years or so. There's just not a mass market for it, though it is well known. My favourite modem edition is from the 1940s, by an English illustrator named Mervyn Peake." She went to a shelf and pulled down a slim yellow volume and handed it to Pinkman.

He thumbed through it. "Strange illustrations," he said.

"Yes, sort of surrealistic Gothic horror," she said. "Peake also did a magnificent *Alice*. I've never been able to find a copy of the first edition of it for sale, and probably even if did I wouldn't be able to afford it!"

"Didn't he write The *Gormenghast* trilogy?" Jinks asked.

"Yes; that's him."

Pinkman looked at him in amazement.

"Hey! I read too!" he protested, silently proud of himself for having recognized the author.

They handed the books back to her. "Thanks very much for taking the time to show them to us," Pinkman said. "They're quite interesting."

"Not at all. It's been my pleasure." Julia left the Catalpa edition lying across the blue carpet and escorted them back to the front door.

"Here's my phone number," Pinkman said, handing her a card. "Give us a call if you see or hear anything suspicious."

"I will."

"Don't open any packages, unless you're certain who sent them," Jinks advised her.

"Why?"

"You never know; it could contain a bomb. I'd say that you're a bit of a high risk target, because of your association with Poole and Snarks."

"I see," she said. "Yes, I'll certainly be careful with the mail from now on," she assured him.

They went back to their car. "Could you believe that? How many copies of *Alice in Wonderland* does a person need, for Pete's sake?" Pinkman said.

"She's obviously a bibliomaniac," Jinks said.

"A what?"

"She's got a neurosis; an obsession with collecting books."

"You just make that up?"

"No, it's a real condition. I read about it once."

"Where? In the *Gormenghast* trilogy?"

"No. I don't remember; *Psychology Today*, maybe."

"You a subscriber?"

"No, I ain't a subscriber! I read them once in a while—while I'm waiting in my dentist's office."

"Are they dangerous?" Pinkman asked.

"Yeah; dentists are real dangerous." He grinned.

"Not dentists, idiot! Bibliomaniacs."

"Not usually. Of course, every once in a while one of them gets into the bomb making business," he said, still grinning.

"In that case, we should have checked her kitchen," Pinkman said.

"For what?"

"Pepper and treacle." They both laughed as they eased out into the traffic.

They made their way across town to Fred Poole's home, a modem brick house with a manicured yard. There were gum trees growing behind it in the backyard and the air was heavy with the fragrance of eucalyptus. There was an old white Volkswagen Rabbit in the driveway, with a vanity plate that read 'I'M LATE.' Mrs. Poole answered the door and invited them in, once they had identified themselves.

"I was just on my way over to the hospital to see my husband," she said as they sat down in the living room.

"What's left of him!" Jinks thought.

"We won't keep you long," Pinkman assured her. "We just wanted to ask you a few questions about your husband."

"I've already told the FBI everything I know about all of this, which is next to nothing. I can't imagine why anyone would want to harm Fred. He's such a dear!"

"Unfortunately, the FBI doesn't always feel obligated to keep us informed of everything they learn. Quite frankly, they regard us at about the same competence level as Barney Fife. But sometimes they miss things."

"I understand. I don't mind talking to you."

"I appreciate that. We understand that your husband is a Lewis Carroll collector."

"Yes. He inherited a collection that his mother started when she was a girl, and he's added to it over the years. He's always been interested in it. He has a number of good friends in the various Carroll societies."

"We talked to Dr. Kerr of the California Chapter and he said that your husband has a large collection of things associated with *The Hunting of the Snark*."

"That's right. It's his favourite book. He quotes from it all the time. 'What I tell you three times is true!' he'll tell me when he really means something. He's always looking for something new to do with it, to add to his collection."

"Would you mind showing us his collection?" Pinkman asked.

"Not at all. He keeps it in his study. I haven't been in there since he was injured, so it might not be too tidy."

"That's not a problem," he assured her.

She led the way and they entered a bedroom that had been converted into a study. The mini-blinds on the windows were closed to block out the sunlight, which could fade the spines of his books. She flipped on the light.

"Oh, my God!" she said.

"What's wrong?" Jinks asked, half expecting to see a body on the floor. "Someone's stolen the paintings!" She pointed at an empty wall and rushed over to it, as if looking closer at the wall might tell her where they had gone. "There were three framed illustrations from an edition of *The Hunting of the Snark* hanging on this wall the last time I was in here! Someone's stolen them! Oh, dear, this will be very upsetting to Fred." Her eyes had filled with tears.

"Were they valuable?"

"Well, yes, to a Carroll collector." She took a Kleenex out of her pocket and dabbed at her eyes. "They were from an edition published recently. Original art, especially anything associated with *The Snark*, is very hard to come by."

"Please look around and see if you can tell if anything else is missing," Pinkman told her.

She scanned the shelves for a few minutes. "Not that I can tell, but Fred knows his collection much better than I do. We probably won't know until he comes home and does an inventory."

"Were the paintings insured?"

"I doubt it. You have to pay a fortune for someone to appraise them in order to get the insurance. He probably thought it was so unlikely that anyone would take them that he didn't bother."

"I'm sorry," Pinkman offered. "Please phone the FPD when you get back from the hospital and report this. They'll send someone out to take the information on the theft and open a case."

"Do you think this might have anything to do with the attempt on Fred's life?" she asked.

"Quite possibly," he said. "But it's hard to say. It is an odd coincidence, though."

"Should I call the FBI and tell them too?"

"That's up to you." He hoped she wouldn't.

"Can you describe the paintings?"

"They were rather garish watercolours, by an artist named Gruszecki; very bright and colourful in the Slavic, surrealistic style one often sees in Czech and Russian children's books. One was a picture of the Bellman standing in the surf. Another was a picture of the Banker being pursued by a dragon-like beast. The last one was of the Baker vanishing away like a Cheshire Cat."

"Actually, I'm having trouble imagining them. Do you happen to have a copy of the edition they were made for?"

"We did. I hope the thief didn't take that, too." She scanned the shelves. "Oh, good! Here it is!" She took it off of the shelf. "This book was hard for Fred to obtain. A friend of his picked it up in Prague when he went through on a business trip a few years ago. He also tracked down the artist through the publisher and got Fred in touch with him to buy the paintings." She leafed through the book to find the pages that were the same as the missing paintings and showed them to the detectives.

"Could you possibly take this by an express copy shop and get colour copies of the missing paintings for us? It might help us find them."

"Of course. I'll do that tomorrow and then drop them by the station for you. Do you really think you can find them?"

"I honestly doubt it. Stolen art can take a long time to resurface. In fact, most of it never does. I wouldn't want to get your hopes up too high; but you never know." They thanked her for talking with them and left.

After weeks of searching the only one of the California *Snark* enthusiasts that they hadn't been able to locate was George Clapham. They had an old address in Canyon Muerta, east of L. A., so they drove out there to look around. They had a hard time locating it. The house was closed up and the yard overgrown with waist-high weeds and brush. "The first time there's a fire through here this place will be gone," Jinks observed as they walked up the dirt drive to the front door. They poked around outside for a while, scaring the lizards, and peered through the dirty windows. They hadn't brought a search warrant, which was just as well.

There was nothing exceptional to see; no sign of anyone having lived in the house for years.

They got in their car and drove back to their motel. Pinkman checked with LAPD, but they had no records on Clapham. They went down to the Denny's next to the motel restaurant to get some lunch. The seated themselves in a booth. It was noon and the place still smelled like breakfast.

"So far all we have is 'a perfect and absolute blank,'" Pinkman said, quoting from *The Snark*.

"Pretty much," Jinks agreed. "Where do we go from here? You got any ideas?"

"Oh, you know me; I've always got ideas. They're not always good ideas, however."

"What have you got at the moment; good, bad or ugly?"

"I was thinking that we might go into Hollywood and visit a few antiquarian book stores to see if anyone's ever dealt with our guy Clapham."

"That might be worthwhile," Jinks agreed. "What else?"

"I've been trying to imagine the bomber, what he might do with himself in his spare time."

"You mean besides torture small animals?"

"Who knows; he might do that, too. I was thinking that he might like to think of himself as a member of the crew of the boat in the poem. You know; he might be a sailor; own a yacht or something. We could check with the Coast Guard and see if there's a boat named 'The Snark' or a boat registered under his name."

"You think he might be that careless, to leave an obvious trail like that?"

"Who knows?"

"Okay, we can do that easy enough. What else?"

"That's it. How about you; you got any ideas yourself?"

"I was wondering if maybe we could set a trap for him by convincing the California Chapter to hold a symposium on *Snarks*. That might well bring him out of cover. I don't see how he could stay away. We could be waiting in the wings and nab him."

"I don't know; we might get some innocent people killed doing that."

Jinks considered this for a moment. "Yeah, I suppose you're right. He might be crazy enough to set off a car bomb and take out the whole Chapter."

"We could ask Dr. Kerr to give us a description of Clapham, since he's met him a few times; we need to put a face on this guy."

The waitress finally showed up. "What can I get you?" she asked Pinkman. "I'll have a piece of bride cake," he said, grinning.

"Yeah, right. Real funny!" she said, though not smiling. "This look like a wedding chapel to you?"

"I don't suppose you have any mutton boiled in sawdust either?" Pinkman asked.

"No," she said, obviously irritated. "The last person who ordered it choked on it and died. The management took it off of the menu. "

"In that case I guess I'll just have to settle for a Caesar salad and a Diet Coke."

"Watching your figure?" she asked. "Good idea!" she added, looking disapprovingly at his paunchy stomach pressed up against the table. "And you, sir?" she said, turning to Jinks.

"I'd really like a nice thick Jub-jub steak," Jinks said, grinning at her.

"You guys are a real riot! Sorry, we're fresh out of Jub-jub. Real popular today."

"Shucks!" said Jinks. "In that case, I guess I'll settle for a double-cheeseburger and fries, with a side of onion rings."

"Everyone's a comedian," she said as she walked away.

"Touchy!" Pinkman said.

After lunch they went into the Coast Guard offices. He identified himself to a clerk, then said, "We're trying to find out if there are any boats named Snark." The clerk laughed hysterically. "You're kidding, right?"

"I'm quite serious. Why's that so funny?"

"SNARK is the world's largest manufacturer of sailboats. There are thousands of them out there. One popular model is the Super Snark."

Pinkman groaned. "Oh. I see what you mean. Well, can you check the registry for anyone named George Clapham?"

"Just a moment. I'll search our database." A few moments later he responded. "Yes. He's got a sailboat that he's named *Snark III*. It's registered in Long Beach."

"Do you have a home address in your database?"

"Yeah; 206 Sea Cliff in San Francisco. I don't know if it's still current, however."

"You want the registration number for the boat?"

"Yes," Pinkman said, and the clerk wrote it down on a piece of paper for him.

They went back to the parking lot.

"Let's go down to Long Beach and see if we can find his boat."

"I just wish I'd brought my trunks" Jinks said grinning broadly.

"Yeah, right; dream on, Alice!"

"You're starting to talk like these people," Jinks said.

Pinkman shrugged. "You're right; this stuff is contagious!"

They drove down to Long Beach and toured around the harbour, which was full of boats. "Just the place for a Snark!" Pinkman said as he parked their car with care.

"Aw, nuts!" Jinks said, stopping and looking up at the sky. "What is it?"

"We forgot to bring the bathing machine!" They laughed as they set off down the wharf to a cluster of moored sailboats. Gulls screamed overhead, angry that they hadn't brought bread.

They spent the entire morning going up and down the harbour, checking the names on sailboats and asking people if they knew George Clapham. They couldn't find the *Snark III*, and they didn't find anyone who would admit to knowing George Clapham.

"You look a bit uffish," Pinkman said. "How about some lunch?"

They walked over to The Walrus and The Carpenter Oyster Bar and ate raw oysters and had a beer, even though they were on duty. Feeling refreshed, they went back to their car then drove north to Hollywood to check out the bookstores.

Their first destination was the Hollywood Hills Bookstore, a small shop that had been designed to look like a bookstore one might see in London, with dark custom made bookcases with locked glass doors. They went in and Pinkman identified himself, asking for the manager.

She came over from where she was sitting at an old roll-top desk at the back of the store. "I'm the manager. May I help you?"

"Perhaps," said Pinkman. He showed her his badge and identified himself, then introduced her to Jinks. "We're looking for a gentleman who might be one of your customers. His name is George Clapham. Do you happen to know him?"

"Yes. He's a regular customer."

"What sort of books is he interested in?" Pinkman asked.

"He always inquires about editions of *The Hunting of the Snark*. That's a nonsense poem by Lewis Carroll, who wrote *Alice's Adventures in Wonderland*."

"I know," Pinkman said.

"I'm sorry; I didn't mean to talk down to you. Not everyone is familiar the poem. *The Hunting of the Snark* seems to be his only interest."

"He had just one idea - and that being 'Snark'," Pinkman said.

"Oh, 1 see that you know the poem very well!"

"Just a few lines. Yes, that would be him. When was the last time he was in your shop?"

"I don't recall an exact date. It was probably within the last month."

"I wonder if you could describe him for me?"

"I'm afraid that I'm not very good at this sort of thing, but I'll try. Let's see; he's middle-aged, thin, with wavy grey hair. He wears wire-rimmed glasses and dresses rather oddly, usually on some nautical theme; a captain's hat, with an anchor crest; that sort of thing. My staff refers to him as Toasted Cheese."

"Why would they do that? I thought Toasted Cheese referred to the Baker."

"My goodness! You're right, of course. You obviously know more than a few lines of the poem. For a policeman, you must be as rare as a Jub-jub's tooth!"

Pinkman grinned. "You wouldn't happen to have his address by any chance?"

"No, I'm sorry; not even a phone number. He's very private, and always pays with cash."

Pinkman was disappointed, but not surprised. "I'd like to send a police sketch artist around and see if you and your staff can help him come up with a likeness. Would that be all right?"

"Of course. Why are you looking for him, if I might ask?"

"We just want to talk with him. He's very difficult to find. You've been a big help today already."

"If he comes in again shall we tell him that you're looking for him?"

"No, that would be a very bad idea. You may find this hard to believe, but he might be quite dangerous. Just give us a call the next time he comes in to your shop." He gave her his card. "If you could manage to get a license plate number when he leaves that would be wonderful, but don't put yourself or your staff at risk."

"Oh, dear," she said.

Then Pinkman added, "You don't happen to have a surveillance camera in the shop do you?" He looked around at the ceiling.

"No, I'm sorry; just a burglar alarm."

"Too bad. I was hoping that you might have caught him on video. The sketch artist should be here tomorrow morning. It shouldn't take him more than an hour. One other thing."

"Yes?"

"Do you have any *Snarks* in stock?"

"Only a few. They sell very quickly. We have a standard first edition in reasonably nice condition. "

"Could I see it?"

"Of course. Just a moment." She went over to a case and unlocked it, then pulled out a book. "Here it is. The spine is a bit sunned and the comers are bumped. But it's a tight, bright copy."

"How much is it?"

She took it back from him and looked at a code penciled on the back endpaper. "Four-hundred dollars."

Pinkman tried not to gasp. "Do you have anything a little less expensive? I was thinking of buying a copy, but I can't afford a week's pay for it."

"Well, we do have a problem copy of the first edition, which is much cheaper."

"What's a problem book?"

"This one is lacking a page, and the condition is generally poor."

"Could I see that one?"

"Of course." She went to an open shelf and came back with a well-worn copy. She opened it and showed him where an illustration had been torn out by someone. "People do this sort of thing, usually to frame an illustration."

"How much is this one?"

"I would be pleased to let you have it for ten dollars," she said.

"Now that's more like it," he said and pulled out his wallet, then paid her.

"Thank you."

"Not at all. I hope that you will enjoy the book."

They said good-bye and left.

"You thinking of becoming a book collector?" Jinks asked once they were outside.

"Yeah. Who knows? I might just join the Lewis Carroll Society."

"Thinking of doing a little undercover snooping?"

"Maybe."

"They'll see right through you, like a biker at a Sunday School picnic."

Two days later Pinkman received the sketch artist's rendering by e-mail. It showed a very nondescript man who could likely blend in almost anywhere if he gave up his nautical garb and tried. The artist had dressed him in a striped sailor's tee shirt; he looked like he'd jumped ship from a Russian destroyer.

George Clapham came into The Hollywood Hills Bookstore two weeks later, wearing his captain's attire, including a dark blue blazer and white turtleneck.

The bookstore's all-female staff went suddenly quiet and as nervous as the Beaver sitting next to the Butcher. George Clapham sensed their tension immediately, making him nearly as nervous as they were.

The Manager was the only one brave enough to come forward to wait on him. "Mr. Clapham; how nice to see you again," she lied in a tremulous tone. "How can we help you today?" She accidentally dropped her glasses and had to stoop to pick them back up, then bumped her knee when she straightened back up.

"Oh, you know me; I'm always searching for *Snarks*;" he said, and then giggled nervously, trying to figure out why she was acting so strange.

"No, no; nothing unusual, I'm afraid. We know your interest, of course, and we always set them aside for your first refusal." Then it occurred to her that she might be able to get his address. "We would be happy to phone you or drop you a note whenever a *Snark* comes in if you will only give us your number or address. It would save you unnecessary trips in to check with us." She smiled as innocently as she could, though she was just about ready to jump out of her skin.

George couldn't get out quickly enough. "That won't be necessary," he said. "I don't mind the trip. Thank you anyway." He bolted for the door, and once outside literally ran, in the opposite direction of where he had parked his car. He ducked into a shop and waited to see if anyone was following him.

The manager phoned Pinkman immediately. "George Clapham was here just a few minutes ago," she told him. "We tried to act normal, but I'm afraid we frightened him. He literally ran out of the bookstore when I asked him for his phone number. I'm sorry."

"It's okay," he assured her. "Thanks for trying." Pinkman knew that George Clapham would never again visit the bookshop, even if a live Snark decided to nest there.

Fit II
Soap

S o a p

*A*lison Cooksley, one of Fresno's most successful real estate agents, came home from showing a house late in the afternoon. When she reached the front door she found a plain white plastic bag hanging from the doorknob. She peeked inside without touching it, now paranoid about bombs, but only saw a free sample of Radiance shampoo in its familiar maroon plastic bottle. She liked the brand. "Good timing!" she thought, as she was nearly out of shampoo. She took it with her into the shower later that evening just before going to bed. She washed off and got the free shampoo bottle. When she twisted the lid the force of the explosion slammed her into the wall of the stall, killing her instantly.

The blast set off her smoke detector and automatically dialled the fire department. Firemen burst through her front door a few minutes later and rushed in to find her crumpled body in the shower, the water still running. They turned off the shower and drug her out onto the bedroom carpet. She had no vital signs, but they spent ten minutes vainly trying to bring her back before giving up and calling for homicide. Since

there had obviously been a bomb they left the house just in case there might be another.

Pinkman and Jinks arrived about fifteen minutes later and made their way through the familiar house to the master bedroom. A patrolman was standing guard at the door to be sure that evidence wouldn't be disturbed. "What can you tell us?" Pinkman asked him.

"There was evidently a bomb. There's a corpse over there on the carpet." He pointed at a body covered by a bedspread. "She died taking a shower. Seems like no where's safe these days!"

"Oh, lots of people die in their bathtubs," Jinks said.

"Not in explosions," he observed.

Pinkman nodded. They went on into the bedroom and the patrolman followed. Pinkman pulled up the comer of the bedspread so they could see her face. It was barely recognizable as a face. Both Pinkman and Jinks winced; the bomb had obviously gone off right in her face. He dropped the corner of the bedspread, having seen more than enough. "I'm pretty certain that this is Alison Cooksley," he said to the patrolman. "She lived here."

The patrolman nodded. "That's what we assumed. You seem to know her."

"Yeah. We interviewed her here a few months back after the Fred Poole bombing. She was a nice lady; too bad!"

Pinkman turned to go into the bathroom and noticed that several of the framed Disney posters nearest to the bathroom had been knocked off of the wall by the force of the explosion.

"Watch your step," the patrolman cautioned. "There's soap all over everything and the tiles are slicker than snot."

"Thanks," Pinkman said and proceeded with a bit more caution. The glass in the vanity mirror and the windows had been shattered. There were shards everywhere.

"Any forks laying around?" Pinkman asked.

The patrolman was surprised by his question. "No; but then most people don't eat in the bathroom."

"Most of the civilized ones don't," Pinkman agreed, as he continued to look around.

"Here's something," he said, squatting down and pointing at a small stainless steel strip

"You think it's important?"

"I'm sure of it."

Another man stuck his head into the bathroom. "ATF Agent Zabrodski," he announced. Pinkman and Jinks stood up and looked at him.

"FPD Detective Pinkman; this is my partner Detective Jinks." They nodded at each other, but didn't shake hands.

"Hi, Jinks," he said and then laughed.

"Kids in Junior High used to say that," Jinks responded. "I used to knock their teeth out."

"That a threat?"

"Take it however you want," Jinks said coolly.

Pinkman interrupted them, pointing out the metal strip to Zabrodski, who produced latex gloves from a coat pocket. He put them on and picked up the metal strip by its edges to examine it.

"What's it say," Pinkman asked.

"They charmed it with smiles and soap."

"That wold be a quote from *The Hunting of the Snark*," Pinkman said.

"Not my idea of charming," Zabrodski replied. "This clearly links this murder to Fred Poole's attempted murder earlier this year."

"Thanks, Sherlock," Jinks said.

"Elementary, my Dear Watson," Zabrodski told him with a sneer. "We'll have a metallurgist compare the two strips."

Evidence technicians soon arrived and began picking through the debris. They scraped up samples of the shampoo, which covered practically everything. They also collected every piece of the plastic bottle they could find, along with any bits of wire and metal.

"Can you please send me a copy of your report?" Pinkman asked Zabrodski.

The agent nodded. "No problem." He paused. "I understand that you two have been investigating the Poole bombing. You come up with anything we should know about?"

"Nothing concrete. We've been concentrating on Poole's associations with the California Chapter of the American Lewis Carroll Society."

"Anything interesting?" he repeated.

"There's one odd guy that we've been looking for who is very hard to find. He acts like he's hiding from the police. Don't know why. He doesn't have a record or any outstanding warrants."

"What's his name?"

"George Clapham."

"You have a photo of him?"

"No, just a police identi-sketch based on descriptions from some of his acquaintances. "

"Send me a copy," Zabrodski said, more like an order than a request.

Pinkman nodded. He'd have to cooperate if he expected him to share things with him.

"What can you tell me about him?"

"He has a keen interest in *The Hunting of the Snark*. So does Fred Poole; and Alison Cooksley, the lady on the carpet in there, did too."

"Why haven't you reported this to the FBI or to us?"

"It's just suspicion on our part; and, up until now, there hadn't been a murder."

"I"d like to come by and talk with you at length about this. You available later this afternoon? Say 3:00?"

Pinkman nodded.

"I'll be there at 3:00, sharp."

Pinkman and Jinks stepped out of the bathroom and left Zabrodski poking around in the broken glass looking for clues. They went over to the bookcases that held Julia's Lewis

Carroll collection, tracking shampoo and little bits of glass across the blue carpet. Pinkman looked for Alison's *Snarks.* "They're gone," he said to Jinks. "Not a snark in sight!"

"You think Poole and Julia were killed for their books?" Jinks asked; the thought seemed ridiculous.

"Well, the books are worth a lot of money, and in this town you can get stabbed for less than five bucks. But, honestly, I doubt it. If someone wanted the books he could have simply burgled the house; no need to set off a bomb and bring the Feds in on top of you. Let's go back to the station and do some brainstorming; see if we can guess who might be the next victim."

"You obviously think there will be another one."

"Likely, I'd say. Don't you think so?"

"Yeah."

When they got back to the station Pinkman and Jinks went into a small conference room with a white board. Pinkman had brought along the problem copy *Snark* that he had bought at the Hollywood Hills Bookstore. He wrote the names of the ten crewmen on the board in a vertical column: Bellman, Boots, Bonnets, Barrister, Broker, Billiard-marker, Banker, Beaver, Baker, and Butcher.

"B seems to have been Carroll's favourite letter," observed Jinks.

"Yeah; just like a kid, he had lots of favourites: the letter B, the number 42, and purple ink. Okay, let's start with Clapham. He's probably the Bellman, based on the way he dresses the part; and he has a sailboat." He wrote his name on the board next to Clapham's.

"Poole could be the Billiard-marker," suggested Jinks. "Pool is an American derivative of billiards."

"A bit obtuse, but possible, I suppose." Pinkman wrote Poole next to Billiard-marker. "Now, Alison Cooksley."

"There weren't any women crewmembers," Jinks pointed out.

"Well, it could have been the Beaver. I imagine that it might be difficult to tell the difference between a male and a female beaver."

"Yeah. After all the Beaver was making lace, which sounds pretty feminine."

"However, Dodgson was a bachelor and didn't seem to care for mature women. A woman was probably the last thing he would want on his imaginary boat destined for a desert isle."

"The logical association would be Baker," said Jinks. "You know: Cook - Baker."

"Of course!" Pinkman penned in her name next to Baker.

"I take it you think that the bomber may be killing off a figurative crew?"

"The thought has occurred to me. What are the names of the other Snark enthusiasts that Dr. Kerr provided?"

Jinks pulled a small notebook out of his shirt pocket and read them off. "Blanche Schwartz, Charlie Barnett, and Julius Imhoff."

"Barnett sounds like 'Bonnets', spoken with a thick accent, so that could be him."

"What about Schwartz? Where's she fit in?"

"Here's a possibility. A boots was someone in Victorian times who blackened and shined a hotel guest's boots while he was sleeping. In German *swarz* means 'black.' So, I'm guessing that's her."

"Yeah, but her first name is Blanche, and *blanc* means 'white' in French," said Jinks.

"It is a strange name; sort of a mixed message."

"Anyway, what about Julius Imhoff? He's an accountant, right?"

"That's right. Perhaps he's either the Broker or Banker."

"Could be." Pinkman wrote Imhoff's name beside both. "That leaves the Barrister. "

"That doesn't seem to fit anyone we've heard of."

"There is someone on the list named Jurist. Let's get back to Dr. Kerr and see if she has any particular interest in *Snarks*."

Agent Zabrodski barged in without knocking. "It's 3:00," he said, which seemed to be his idea of a greeting.

"Take a chair," Pinkman suggested.

"Hi, Jinks," he said, then laughed.

Jinks had a difficult time controlling his anger. "Agent Broad-asski," Jinks replied as an acknowledgement. Zabrodski glared at him, but let it go. "What have you got for me?" he asked, as if Pinkman and Jinks worked for him.

"We were just summarizing it here on the board." Pinkman explained their theory.

"Based on this, you think Clapham is the bomber?"

"Could be; he's our prime suspect."

"I think you guys are in danger of losing your jobs, if not your minds. This is the biggest load of crap I've ever seen."

Pinkman and Jinks didn't respond at first, put off by his reaction to their theory. "I realize that it does seem a bit far-fetched," Pinkman admitted.

"A bit? What's the motive?"

"We aren't sure. Could be he's just a psycho. I guess we won't know if there's anything to any of this unless someone else on this list gets hit."

"What do you propose to do now?" Zabrodski asked, the tone of his voice still incredulous.

"We need to find George Clapham. The FBI could assist in that. Everyone on this list needs to be warned that his or her lives might be in danger."

"On the strength of that?" asked Zabrodski, pointing at the board. "Not a chance." He got up and left; didn't even say good-bye.

They were silent for a minute. "Perhaps he's right," Pinkman finally said. "I wish now that we had never explained our theory. He seems to think everything we do on this case is a big joke."

"Let's don't let him get us down. The ATF and FBI aren't making any noticeable progress, so they aren't nearly as smart as they act. Let's just do what we know to do and if someone gets hurt then it won't be because of any negligence on our part."

"You're right."

The crime lab report on Alison Cooksley came in a few days later. Once again the explosive in the device had been Semtex, the Czechoslovakian equivalent to C-4. The shampoo was ordinary stuff, available in half of the drugstores and supermarkets in the country. The bomber had taken great care to carefully scratch away the identifying codes on the plastic bottle.

Jinks had been on the phone. "Dr. Kerr says Rachel Jurist does have quite a number of *Snarks* in her collection. He gave me her phone number."

"Why don't you give her a call and just ask her to be especially careful, but try not to panic her."

Fit III
Spadework

Spadework

George Clapham was a very paranoid individual. He had just learned a few weeks ago, from the owner of the Long Beach Marina, that two policemen were trying to locate him. Then, when the manager at the Hollywood Hills Bookstore had tried to get him to give her his address and phone number he panicked. He put his Lewis Carroll collection in vaulted, environmentally controlled storage, packed his bags and went to his country home in the hills west of Los Angeles to lay low. He imagined all sorts of people looking for him besides the police: his former wife, Mafia hit men, secret agents, and even aliens. He really believed it was probably the latter. Ever since his painful abduction experience three years ago he imagined these terrifyingly cruel little grey creatures behind practically every bush. Who knew? Perhaps they had even infiltrated the police departments. He wasn't about to let them find him again and perform any more excruciatingly painful experiments on his brain and sexual organs.

He was glad now that he had sold his sailboat. He would miss it, but knew that if someone tried hard enough they could probably trace him through it. When he arrived in L.A. he went straight to a Goodwill store and donated all of his nautical garb, including his collection of captain's hats. He didn't have any use for them any more without the boat, and he felt they made him look too conspicuous.

The house in the canyon was a mess since no one had lived in it in years. It would take him weeks to get it cleaned up to liveable standards. All of the stuffed furniture would have to be thrown out since mice had taken them over. And he would need a new bed and refrigerator. He decided to wait until tomorrow to go into town and buy new ones. He would spend the night in the RV he had driven. He was too exhausted to start cleaning, and went to bed early.

He awoke in the middle of the night to the sound of someone banging on the side door. He fumbled for the overhead light and checked the time. It was 2:30 a.m. The banging continued, but he was too terrified to see who it was or to find out what they wanted. The banging stopped momentarily, then he heard the terrible metallic sounds of the door being pried open with a crowbar. In a few moments the door flew open and a figure dressed entirely in black and wearing a ski mask entered the van carrying a spade.

The Snark said nothing and went straight to Clapham, who was sitting upright in bed, frozen in terror, like Scrooge awaiting the arrival of the next ghost. It took his attacker three hard blows to the head to kill him with the shovel, and by the time the attack was over the bed was awash with blood, which was also splattered across the walls and ceiling. Once back in L.A., the Snark stopped off at a pay phone and placed a call to LAPD, telling them where to find the body.

Pinkman first heard about the murder while watching the evening news. He called Jinks and they met at the station.

They began making inquiries to get the details, requesting a copy of the case and autopsy reports. The police report arrived within a few minutes on the fax, and they studied it together. There was no indication that LAPD had yet related the murder to the two Fresno bombings. The cause of death was a fractured skull and loss of blood. The murder weapon, a WW II foxhole shovel, available in hundreds of Army surplus stores, had been dropped outside Clapham's RV in plain view. The murderer had honed the shovel's edge to paring knife sharpness.

"The Boots and the Broker were sharpening a spade," Pinkman told Jinks, quoting from *The Hunting of the Snark*.

"So much for our theory that Clapham was the bomber," Jinks replied.

"Yeah; bummer. Well, we had tentatively identified Schwartz as the Boots," Pinkman said. "The poem might imply that she's our most likely suspect, since the Boots was the one who helped sharpen the spade. Schwartz is a stockbroker, isn't she?"

Jinks pulled out his notes. "She's a broker, she's a broker, she's a broker!" Jinks declared.

"Very funny."

"One thing that bothers me though is that the killer didn't leave his signature metal strip with a Snarkian quote. "

"Perhaps the killer thought it would be obvious from the cause of death. After all, the murder weapon was left in plain view. The killer obviously wanted it to be found."

"Maybe." Pinkman heard the fax, and got up to see if it was for them. "Here's the autopsy report on Clapham. Here we go! There was a plate! The pathologist found it in Clapham's mouth when he opened it to examine his teeth to confirm his identity against dental records. Guess what's inscribed on it?"

"Oh, I'm sure it's your quote about sharpening a spade."

"Right on!" Pinkman was proud of himself, and grinned broadly.

Detective Cox came over to their desks, carrying a newspaper. "You guys seen today's paper?" he asked. He handed it to Pinkman; Jinks looked over his shoulder.

SECOND GRISLY "SNARK" MURDER
Victim Encounters a Boojum

Los Angeles (UPI) - Local area resident George Clapham was found brutally murdered at his vacation home in Canyon Muerta in west L.A. yesterday.

LAPD reports that the cause of death was multiple blows to the head. The murder weapon, a foxhole shovel, has been recovered.

The autopsy revealed that his assailant inserted an engraved metal plate in his victim's mouth, with a quote from an obscure nonsense poem, *The Hunting of the Snark*, by Lewis Carroll, author of *Alice's Adventures in Wonderland*. The FBI says that this quote links his murder to two unsolved bombings in Fresno earlier this year, one of which was fatal. According to Dr. Grant Kerr, President of the California Chapter of the American Lewis Carroll Society (ALCS), the poem, first published in 1876, is a surrealistic tale of a crew of nine men and a beaver who set sail to an uncharted island in search of mystical creatures called Snarks.

According to Dr. Kerr, there are several different varieties of Snark, including one called a Boojum, which is invariably fatal when encountered. "You simply vanish away" he said.

Dr. Kerr confirmed that George Clapham, along with the two Fresno bombing victims, Fred Poole and Alison Cooksley , was a member of the California Chapter of the ALCS, and that all three were *Snark* enthusiasts and collectors.

Boojum is the name of a grotesque desert plant found in the Sonoran Desert, apparently named by its discoverer after this particularly lethal species of Snark, which for some reason he thought it resembled.

They were still reading the newspaper when Zabrodski stormed in. "Let's talk," he said to Pinkman and Jinks. "You got a private office we can go to?"

"We can use one of the interrogation rooms," Pinkman said as he got up. They all went down the hall to the room. "What can we do for you?" Pinkman asked when they had seated themselves.

"You've heard about George Clapham, I suppose."

"Yes."

"The last time I was here you two had a screwball theory about the Fresno bombings. Frankly, I thought you were nuts. But there obviously was a link between them, though, as I recall, you had postulated that Clapham might be the bomber. He evidently wasn't. I'd like to see the chart you had drawn on the board the last time I was here."

"My notes are back at my desk. It'll just take me a moment to get them." Pinkman left to retrieve them, grinning all the way. When he got back he wrote it all out on the white board again, and this time Agent Zabrodski took notes.

"So, as I understand this, you two believe that the killer might be Blanche Schwartz?"

"It's possible," said Jinks.

"Who else might be the killer?"

"It could logically be anyone in the ALCS, not necessarily someone from their California Chapter. So far, we've been working on the obvious assumption that it's someone who has a specific interest in *The Hunting of the Snark*."

"Have you guys interviewed Schwartz?"

"We talked to her some months ago by phone. The conversation was normal. She didn't give us any reason to believe she might be a bomber. We thought at the time that it was more likely that she was a potential victim and were just cautioning her to be careful. You might want to talk to her yourself," Pinkman said. "The FBI interviewed her as well."

"I'll look into that."

"Anything else?" Pinkman asked.

"No. Just let me know if you find any more links or associations will you? You have my number, right?"

"We've got it," Pinkman assured him

Agent Zabrodski got up and stormed out.

"Well," Jinks said. "We don't seem to be regarded as quite so full of crap as the last time."

They went back to their desks, and Pinkman found that he had a message to phone Dr. Kerr. He placed the call and the doctor came to the phone.

"Dr. Kerr," Pinkman said. "You called?"

"Yes. I wonder if we might talk the next time you're in the Los Angeles area? It's nothing urgent. I'd just like to see where the case is going. It's having a rather negative impact on our Society."

"Of course. Actually, as it happens, my partner and I are driving down to L.A. this afternoon anyway."

"In that case, perhaps you might drop by my home later this evening, about 7:00?"

"That will be fine."

"I'll see you then. I may not be punctual, since the traffic is hard to predict. You have the address, I believe. "

"That's not a problem. Yes, we have your address. Thank you. Good-bye."

Pinkman hung up. "Dr. Kerr wants to talk to me this evening at 7:00 at his home. I told him we were going down to L.A. this afternoon."

"We are?"

"I just told him that; I've been wanting to interview him anyway, and this is a good excuse. You want to join me? Could be interesting."

"Of course."

"If we leave now we can get there by 6:00, and we can grab a bite to eat somewhere."

Fit IV
Special Collections

Special Collections

*B*arbara Wilson had married Grant Kerr immediately
after he graduated from Harvard Medical and Dental
Schools. He had then accepted an internship and residency
in paediatric oral surgery at John Hopkins, and three years
later they had moved to Los Angeles where Grant joined a
paediatrics practice. He had become wealthy beyond reason.

It was, no doubt, in large part his love for children that had
also led him to an equally strong love for children's literature.
He had collected a number of children's authors for years
before finally discovering Lewis Carroll. He had sold all of his
earlier collections to Justin Thriller in New York, for a
substantial profit, and used the money to begin building what
was to become one of the world's greatest private Lewis
Carroll collections.

Babs, as all of her friends called her, didn't share Grant's
love of either *Alice* or Lewis Carroll, but tolerated it simply
because the books and society acquaintances seemed to make
him so happy. In the beginning, at least, if they made Grant
happy they made her happy. However, images of the Rev.

Charles Dodgson photographing little nude girls were too much for her more modern, though otherwise liberal, sensibilities. She was amazed that the world was so willing to overlook his behaviour simply because he had written the *Alice* books.

Things had gradually turned for the worst with the founding of the California Chapter of the American Lewis Carroll Society. Naturally enough, Grant had been a founding member, and he had held every one of the society's offices, except Treasurer, at least once. The society often met in their palatial Brentwood mansion, But just because one had the facilities to entertain forty guests, didn't mean that one had to enjoy the meetings, which she usually found excruciatingly boring. Silly papers about whether or not Queen Victoria or Mark Twain was the true author of *Alice in Wonderland*, or elaborate analyses of the printing variations of the tails of mice, were more than she could stand, and she usually left shortly after the meetings got started.

Over the years Grant had become so obsessed with Carroll that he had developed full-blown bibliomania. It was not an uncommon neurosis in California, where people seemed to have the necessary money to invest in all sorts of expensive things, from antique automobiles to the old clothing of movie stars. Most people could hardly afford $15,000 for an Appleton *Alice* or $30,000 for an original Dodgson photographic print of a young girl dressed up like Little Red Riding Hood; but Grant could, and often did. The halls of their mansion had fifteen framed Dodgson photographs, all fitted with little dark green velvet curtains, which served to block the harmful rays of light, which would tend to fade the antique prints. She felt it was absurd to live with so many pictures that you couldn't even see unless you pulled back a curtain. Somehow it always reminded her of Dodgson hiding behind the dark curtain of his tripod mounted camera, peering through the lens at upside-down little nude girls.

Babs also gradually began to resent the enormous amount of money he spent on his omnivorous collecting, but even more the time he spent with his books, and meeting the Society's endless demands. She felt like she had gradually lost her husband to some ghostly and beautiful virtual Victorian mistress.

Pinkman and Jinks arrived promptly at 7:00 at the Kerr's Brentwood mansion. Babs had been expecting them and met them at the door. "Good evening, gentlemen. I assume that you're from the Fresno Police Department?"

"Yes. My name is Detective Pinkman; this is my partner Detective Jinks." Jinks nodded at her.

"I'm Barbara Wilson-Kerr. Please, come in," she said, opening the door wide and stepping back to let them in.

They stepped into a spacious foyer that seemed cold enough to keep meat from spoiling. Pinkman's first thought was to wonder how anyone could possibly afford the electricity bill; he was glad that he had on a sports jacket. The foyer was graced by an elegantly abstract Brancusi bronze bust, perched atop a polished black marble pedestal on one wall and an Andy Warhol portrait of Marilyn Monroe opposite. Marilyn was flanked by two small-framed pictures, which were covered by dark green curtains. Pinkman wanted to go over and peek to see what they were hiding, but resisted the impulse.

"I'm afraid that Grant is delayed. He phoned a few minutes ago and said that he was on his way, but would be about fifteen minutes late. That's typical for doctors, you know; there's always some crisis or other."

"That's not a problem," Pinkman assured her.

"Good. Please come and sit down." She led the way into a huge living room with no fewer than five sectional sofas arranged around several coffee tables. Huge potted plants decorated the room, and large abstract paintings adorned the walls. "Would either you care for a glass of wine or a cup of coffee while you wait?"

"No thank you." Pinkman said, afraid that he might spill it on the white carpet. Jinks also declined. They all sat down, opposite each other.

"I assume that you're here to talk with Grant about these terrible murders," Barbara said, trying to make conversation.

"Yes. We're hopeful that your husband will be able to help us in our investigation. "

"I don't see how he possibly could."

"Oh, he's been very helpful already," Pinkman assured her. "As you probably know from all of the press, the murders and bombings are connected to Lewis Carroll."

"It's just terrible!" she said. "Some crazy person out these killing these harmless people just because they happen to like *Alice in Wonderland*."

"Actually, the connection seems to be with *The Hunting of the Snark*, not *Alice*," Pinkman responded.

"Whatever. Do you have any suspects?"

"Well, I suppose everyone in the American Lewis Carroll Society could be considered a suspect."

"Even Grant?" she asked, her face expressing shocked disbelief at such a possibility.

"We're not actively investigating your husband. Actually, he called us, and wanted to talk."

"Well, I can assure you that Grant is not a serial killer!"

"Of course not. We have no reason to think that your husband is a serial killer," Pinkman assured her. "Quite the contrary, he's been very helpful and cooperative. I was just talking in generalities."

She smiled weakly.

"Oh! Here's Grant now," she exclaimed, as Grant Kerr walked into the room. "I'm terribly sorry to be late. It was unavoidable, I'm afraid. A teenage boy wasn't wearing his seatbelt and tried to remove the windshield with his front teeth."

Pinkman and Jinks stood up. "It's no problem at all," Pinkman assured him. "We've enjoyed a nice conversation with your wife."

"Please, be seated," Dr. Kerr said, gesturing at the couch they had just gotten up from.

"You'll please excuse me," Babs said. "I'm late for my karate class. It's been nice talking with you, gentlemen." She smiled and left the room.

"Your wife takes karate?" Jinks asked, surprised that a middle-aged woman would be doing that.

"She's a bit of an orientalist and very athletic. She also practices yoga and Thai Chi, and does Japanese flower arranging and brush painting. She's quite talented; very clever with her hands."

Pinkman tried to imagine her shattering cinder blocks with her bare hands, but couldn't. "What did you want to talk to us about?" he asked, changing the subject. "As you can imagine," Dr. Kerr replied, "these terrible bombings and murders have had a very negative impact on our California Chapter of the American Lewis Carroll Society."

"I'm sure they don't help," Pinkman agreed.

"To put it mildly! Over half of our members have quit out of fear that they might be one of the killer's next targets. Most collectors have put their *Snarks* up for auction on e-Bay or have offered them to antiquarian booksellers; they're available for a song. Our next meeting is at UCLA and the university has had to beef up security because of us."

"That would seem to be prudent, under the circumstances," Pinkman said. "I imagine that their insurers probably put up a fuss about it."

"Exactly. I suppose I can't blame them."

"What did you want to talk to us about?" Pinkman asked.

"How close are you to catching this maniac?" he asked.

"All we have at the moment is a rather obtuse theory."

"Which is?"

"I'm afraid I can't discuss that. It might jeopardize our investigation."

"Of course; I understand. I shouldn't have even asked. It's just that if the police don't catch this person soon the California Chapter will dissolve out of fear. That would be a great tragedy. It's taken many years and a great deal of work to get it established."

"Yes, sir. I'm sure that it has. I can assure you that we are doing everything we know to do; and it's not just the Fresno Police. LAPD has a task force, as does the FBI and ATF. Some of the best investigative minds in the country are involved. I'm sure it's just a matter of time until the perpetrator is caught."

"Is there anything I can do to speed up that process?" Kerr asked.

"I can't think of anything right now."

"I was wondering if there might be some way to set a trap for the killer," Kerr said.

"Like what?" Jinks asked.

"Oh, I don't know; perhaps at a chapter meeting, or something."

"I don't think that would be too good of an idea. It would put those in attendance at great risk. But we'll keep that in mind, if something makes sense. Thank you for offering. "

"Not at all. I desperately want you to apprehend this guy!"

"Are you also dumping your own *Snark* collection?" Jinks asked.

"Oh, no! I'd never do that! You'd have to pry them out of my cold, dead fingers," he said as a joke, then laughed. "Quite the contrary, actually; I've been buying most of the copies that are coming onto the market. It's a once in a lifetime opportunity."

"How many editions have you got now?" Pinkman asked.

"I'm not sure; something over six hundred."

"Can we see them?" Jinks asked.

"Of course! I'm always happy to show my collection. It's back this way." He got up, and Pinkman and Jinks followed.

"I'll have to turn off the alarm and fire protection systems. It'll just take a moment." He left, retreating into a hallway, and then returning shortly.

"The library has a rather sophisticated burglar alarm system, and a Halon fire suppression system. In the event of a fire the room is automatically flooded with an inert gas to smother combustion by depleting the oxygen."

"Wouldn't that kill you if you were in the library?"

"Of course. You only have about ten or fifteen seconds to get out of the room when a fire alarm sounds."

"That seems a bit risky," Jinks said.

"It's a necessary precaution. The books are not only valuable, but many items are unique and irreplaceable. It would be completely unacceptable to have them go up in smoke."

"What if the fire just comes through the walls from somewhere outside the room?"

"The library has eight-hour fire walls," Dr. Kerr replied. "That's not too likely."

They went inside. The room was window-less, perhaps twenty-five foot square. The air was cool and dry. Lighting was indirect and subdued. Three walls were covered, floor to ceiling, with bookcases, all completely full. Rows of lower bookcases filled the middle of the room, like those in a public library. There was a desk, with a PC and a lamp, and several adjacent filing cabinets. A large glass case, that reminded Pinkman of the trophy case outside a university gymnasium, covered the fourth wall; it was filled with figurines, dolls, and a wild assortment of *Alice* ephemera: wristwatches, jewellery, dishes, glasses, etc. Stacks of books sat on most of the available floor space between the bookcases.

"I'm going to have to expand the room. As you can see, I'm running out of space."

"This must be the largest Lewis Carroll collection in the world," Pinkman said.

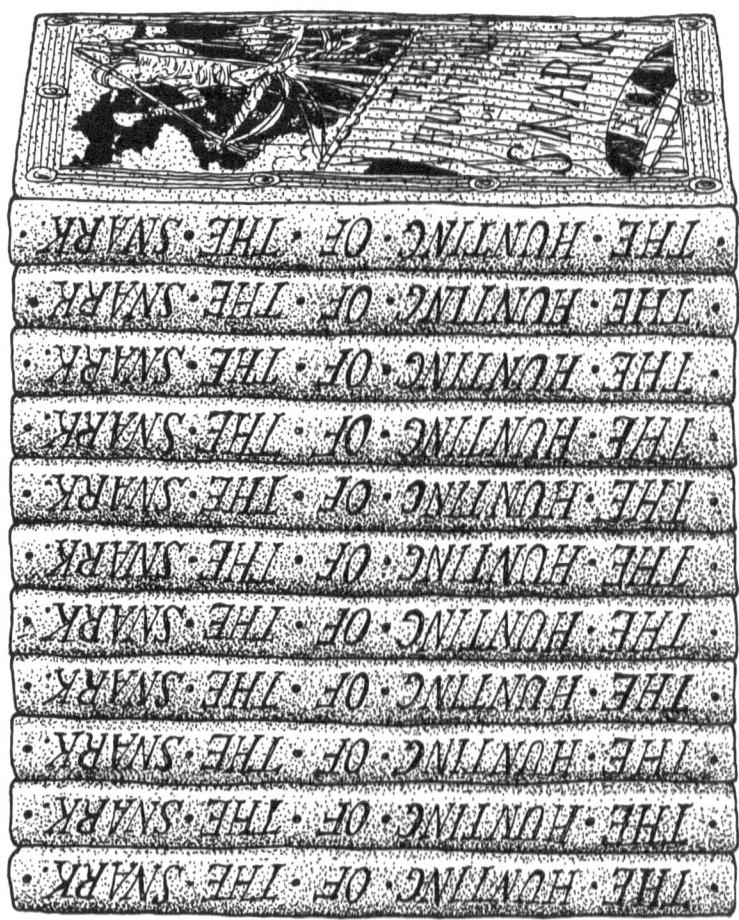

"I doubt it, but without doubt it's one of the largest," Kerr said. "Most of the *Snarks* are over this way," he said, stepping over and around stacks of books. Pinkman and Jinks followed.

The collection was impressive. "We've seen the *Snark* collections owned by Poole and Cleaver. They were quite small compared to this," Pinkman said. "Aren't you afraid that this collection makes you a prime target for the killer?"

"Oh, I'm sure he wouldn't want to kill me. Why would he want to? I'm nice to everyone."

"As far as I know, Poole and Schwartz were nice to everyone, too. I don't think that absolves you of the risk."

"Did you ever see Clapham's collection?" Kerr asked.

"No one's been able to locate it. He must have it hidden away somewhere; perhaps under another name. He was very secretive. Who knows? It may never surface."

"That would be a pity!" said Kerr. "A very big pity! I'd like very much to acquire it from his estate."

"Well, thank you for showing us your collection. It's quite impressive," Pinkman said. "Unless you have something else, I think we'll be driving on back to Fresno."

"No, no; I don't have anything else in mind."

As they were leaving Jinks bent over and looked at one of the stacks of books on the floor. They were all various editions of *The Hunting of the Snark*.

They said good night and left.

"That was very strange," Pinkman said.

"One thing's for sure; the guy sure has lots of money!"

"That's an understatement. His book collection must be worth millions."

"I wouldn't be surprised. But that pales in comparison to his house."

"I'd guess at least fifteen million."

"It seems to me that we have to start thinking of Dr. Kerr as a suspect," Pinkman said.

"Yeah, I agree. He has the money to do anything he wants. Did you notice that those stacks of books on the floor were all editions of the *Snark*?"

"No, but I'm not surprised. This whole situation makes it very easy to acquire them cheaply and in huge numbers."

"Are you thinking that he might be perpetrating the murders as a way of acquiring the books?"

"It's a possibility."

"A bit extreme, but the same thought occurred to me."

"Yeah, and besides, the guy's a bibliomaniac. Who knows what he's capable of doing in order to get his hands on more books?"

"What'd you think of his wife, Barbara?"

"I wouldn't want to meet her in a dark alley!" They both laughed.

The next morning Cox came by their desks with the morning newspaper. "You guys see this?" he asked, tossing it to Pinkman.

"You seem to have taken on a newspaper route," Jinks told him. "The Department not paying you enough?"

"Just trying to be helpful," Cox said, grinning. Pinkman looked at page three:

SERIAL KILLER STILL AT LARGE
FBI Contacting Carrollians in Hunt for "Boojum" Snark

Washington, DC (UPI) - An FBI spokesman confirmed today that FBI and ATF agents have begun interviewing all present and past members of the American Lewis Carroll Society (ALCS) in a desperate nationwide hunt for the serial killer, dubbed by the press as the "Boojum" Snark. Members of the literary society are outraged that they have come under suspicion. Parents of school children who are members are particularly upset, protesting that the interviews are upsetting their children, whose grades have begun to suffer.

Well over half of the current ALCS members have panicked and cancelled their memberships.

Fred Poole, the killer's first victim, is still recovering from his wounds that cost him an eye and a finger. "I've sold my collection," Mr. Poole told UPI yesterday. "I'm not willing to die over some silly children's books."

Mr. Poole evidently isn't alone. E-Bay on-line auction has hundreds of editions of *The Hunting of the Snark* listed, as collectors dump their holdings of Lewis Carroll's nonsense poem out of fear of becoming the "Boojum" Snark's next victim.

Rob Duckworth, current President of the ALCS, spoke to UPI by phone from his home in Maryland. "The Society wishes to offer its condolences to the families of the victims. We hope and pray that this dastardly killer is caught and brought to justice with all speed." He denies rumours that the ALCS plans to disband. "Our next quarterly meeting at the Harry Ransom Humanities Research Center (HRHRC) at the University of Texas at Austin (UTA) will go ahead as planned, and we hope that everyone will attend."

UTA Police spokesman Jim Baca confirmed to UPI that extraordinary security precautions would be in place for the upcoming Austin meeting. "We plan to shoot Snarks on sight," he joked. "Anyone entering the building the day of the meeting will have to pass through a metal detector and we will have a bomb sniffing dog on hand."

Two of the serial killer's victims, Alison Cooksley of Fresno and George Clapham of Los Angeles, died in separate attacks earlier this year.

"Dr. Kerr's worst fears," Pinkman said.
"Or fondest hopes," Jinks said; "could go either way."

Babs was literally hot blooded, her body temperature normally hovering a few degrees above normal. Anyone else would have thought they were suffering from a fever.

Because of this physiological oddity she was invariably uncomfortable with the room temperature. She set the thermostat for the house low enough to be just bearable, though most people found it much too cold. She also found it impossible to sleep unless the room temperature was somewhere below fifty degrees; even then, she often slept nude or with only a sheet as a cover. They had installed an industrial five-ton air conditioning unit just for her large four-room bedroom suite, and she ran it hard. She even took cold showers. Grant didn't normally go into her frigid suite, and on the rare occasion when he did he usually pulled on a sweater. He sometimes felt that she ran it so cold just to drive him away.

One of the reasons he had married her was that he loved her hot skin; it made sex all the more exciting when it was easy to imagine that she had warmed to his touch, even though that had almost nothing to do with it. However, in spite of her Latin body temperature, her libido had cooled and since it was close to Valentine's Day he had decided to try to put some spark back into their love life. He had bought her an expensive piece of antique Japanese calligraphy, but had also been shopping the Internet for very sexy lingerie that he would like to see her in, though he realized that it was problematic as to whether or not he could get her to wear it. He was hoping that the calligraphy would warm her to the idea. All he needed was to confirm her bra size.

Babs was out for the afternoon, so he pulled on a sweater and went into her suite. It was so cold in her bedroom that he was amazed that he couldn't see his breath. He went into one of her walk-in closets, which felt like cold storage, and started opening drawers until he found one with bras in it. As he was fumbling around with the bras he noticed the comer of a manila envelope beneath them, and out of curiosity took it out to see what was in it.

He opened the envelope and pulled out a large book, which he immediately recognized as a copy of the Catalpa Press edition of *The Hunting of the Snark*. "What's this!" he exclaimed in his mind. "What an amazing thing to find in her lingerie drawer! Oh, I get it. She's been buying Valentine presents too! She probably doesn't know that I already have at least thirty copies of this one. Still, it's a very sweet thought!" He smiled and slipped it back inside the envelope without looking at the very familiar book and put it back where he had found it. He checked the tag on a few bras, then closed the drawer and left her suite.

Fit V
The Snark Club

The Snark Club

*B*abs opened the lingerie drawer where she kept the Catalapa Press edition of *The Hunting of the Snark*. Something immediately didn't look quite right to her; she had the impression that someone had been rummaging through the drawer. She looked closely, but finally decided that it had probably just been her maid, Maria, and put it out of her mind.

She took the book out of its manila envelope and laid it on the thick carpet. She pulled out its crazy first chapter, which stretched the length of the closet. She had scrawled the surnames of ten members of the California Chapter across the faces in the illustration with a red Magic Marker: Clapham on the Bellman; Schwartz on the Boots; Barnett on the Maker of Bonnets and Hoods; Jurist on the Barrister; Imhoff on the Broker; Poole on the Billiard-marker; Constantinescu on the Banker; Castor on the Beaver; Cooksley on the Baker; and, Cleaver on the Butcher. In addition, the faces of both the Billiard-marker and the Baker had bold black X's across their faces. She didn't have anything personal against any of them;

69

she had simply selected them because of their names or occupations.

She got down on her knees and slashed a large X across the face of the Bellman with a ballpoint pen, wielding it like a dagger and puncturing the thick paper in the process. "You should have followed the Baker's advice and procured your own second-hand dagger-proof coat!" she said, as if the little man in the illustration could hear her. She stood up and studied the long nonsensical boat for a few minutes, trying to decide how to kill the next crewman. She folded the chapter back up, then returned the book to its hiding place beneath the stack of expensive bras, many decorated with lace so delicate that the Beaver could have made it.

Julia Castor was a great Carroll enthusiast, though she much preferred *Alice* to *Snarks*. Nonetheless, she was one of the founding members of the secretive Snark Club, and hadn't missed one of its annual meetings in thirty years. The exclusive club always met in a private dining room at the Hotel del Coronado in San Diego for a seafood dinner.

It was a pleasant drive from L. A. to San Diego, where the weather was invariably nicer; and there was typically less smog, though she could remember twice when it had been just as bad as L. A. The dinner was always at 8:00 p.m., but she went early and checked into the hotel by 4:00, just ahead of the heaviest rush-hour traffic. That gave her plenty of time for a nice walk around the bougainvillea bedecked hotel grounds, and a cocktail before dinner.

She timed herself to arrive at the meeting exactly at 8:00 and found the other seven remaining members of the club already there. She went round and greeted them all. Their mood was subdued, even a bit sombre, in light of recent events that had cost the lives of two of their long-time crew, Alison Cooksley and George Clapham.

The Bellman, a title held by Roger Bellamy ever since the founding of the club, rang an antique hand bell that had once been used aboard ship by the captain of a four-masted schooner. He always started the meeting this way. The crewmembers took their places at the sound, sitting wherever they liked. Membership in the Snark Club was strictly limited to ten members, and in the event one of them died or resigned, the remaining crew would elect a replacement, who would be contacted, sworn to secrecy and invited to join. No one had ever declined his or her invitation. Each member was assigned the name of one of the crew, which he or she retained for life or until they resigned, though no one had ever resigned. Julia held The Snark Club's position of Baker.

The table was set with three forks, but no spoon or knife, as befitted their Snarkian quest. As soon as they were seated the waiters came in with *Gambas at Ajillo* as their first course. The air was soon filled with the strong aroma of garlic. This was followed by a snapper *Bourride*, then *Kalamarakia Tiganita me Skothalia*. Now there really was a strong smell of garlic in the air! Next came *Cozze Arrosto*, with exceptionally large mussels, and finally *Latte alla Grotta*. A waiter brought in cognac and Kamal Biswas magically produced a box of $50 Cuban cigars that he had smuggled in from a recent trip to Montreal (where he had searched diligently for French *Alices*), and passed them around. Julia lit up with the rest of them. The cigar smoke finally overwhelmed the piercing smell of garlic.

The Bellman stood up to speak. He was dressed in his traditional costume that made him look very much like Henry Holiday's illustration of the character. He produced a prized miniature edition of *The Hunting of the Snark*, which had been custom bound in alligator in the 1920s, which he opened and read from:

"We should all of us grieve, as you well may believe,
 If you never were met with again—
But surely, my man, when the voyage began,
 You might have suggested it then?

"It's excessively awkward to mention it now—
 As I think I've already remarked."
And the man they called "Hi!" replied, with a sigh,
 "I informed you the day we embarked.

"You may charge me with murder—"

"I know that all of you share my great sadness at the tragic demise of our Butcher, Alison Cooksley, and our Beaver, George Clapham, taken from our midst by a cowardly murderer. We can only hope that the police will apprehend this monster quickly, and that none of us will become his next victim. He's as deadly as a Bandersnatch, and each of you must take special precautions for your own safety!"

The crew murmured.

"Since the first victim of the bomber wasn't one of our crew I assume that this psychopath hasn't somehow singled us out. However, the very fact that Alison and George were victims and that we are associated with the *Snark*, necessarily puts us all at high risk. You were all as courageous as the Baker in attending tonight. I'm just thankful that we have judiciously elected to keep our club's very existence a secret; that's probably our best protection. Even a second-hand dagger-proof coat is no match for a bomb!"

Dr. Kamal Biswas, the Club's Banker, interrupted the Bellman to say, "I can offer two excellent Policies, one Against Fire and one Against Damage from Hail."

Everyone laughed softly with relief at his small joke. Things were getting too grim and serious; these meetings were supposed to be fun.

"So, the first order of business is to nominate a replacement Butcher and a Beaver," the Bellman continued with his speech, looking grand, as always.

Julia stood up. "Captain, I nominate Wanda Kerley to be the Beaver. It would certainly be nice to keep another female on board, if at all possible. I'm not at all sure how safe a lone woman might be on a deserted isle with the likes of this crew."

Everyone giggled. Julius Imhoff, the Broker, stood up and said, "I'd like to remind you that Mr. Dodgson had the good sense to keep women off of the ship." He grinned. "We just made an exception for you and Alison, because you're such good cooks, and we get tired of eating nothing but bridecake."

Julia smiled back at him, then continued, "Wanda Kerley is a great Carrollian and Snarkist. And you're right; she makes excellent cheesecake." Having said this she started to sit down, but stood right back up. "Did I tell you that she makes excellent cheesecake?" She then sat down, only to pop up again. "Some of you might like to keep in mind when you're casting your ballots that Wanda makes excellent cheesecake!"

The Broker stood back up and said, "In spite of the fact that it's been established beyond any doubt that Wanda Kerley makes excellent cheesecake, I'd like to nominate Dr. Grant Kerr as the Beaver. This makes perfect sense, since he's a Canadian immigrant. As is well known, the beaver is his native country's national symbol and no one has ever been as busy as he has. Why, he's held every office in the California Chapter of the Society except one, some of them twice and one even thrice. He can recite *The Hunting of the Snark* from memory and even knows the first stanza backwards, something that I certainly can't do. He has also composed dozens of very funny limericks that involve Snarks. He has a pet Boojum Tree in his sunroom. I'm happy to report that he eats with a fork and frequently uses soap. His only drawbacks are that he's quite bald and not very furry, like a beaver should be; his tail is quite flat, however."

Everyone clapped and laughed, and the Captain tingled his bell. "Speaking of limericks," he said:

"A Butcher once took up his cleaver,
And decided to murder the Beaver,
* The Beaver took flight,*
* And was soon out of sight,*
So the Butcher wasn't able to eat her."

The crewmen laughed and the Bellman took a little bow. The Banker stood up. "Have you heard this one?" he asked:

"There once was a troublesome Snark,
Who frightened the crew as a lark;
* It hid in a chasm,*
* Screamed like a phantasm,*
Till the crew sailed away in their barque."

"Are there any other limericks or nominations?" asked the Bellman. The Broker stood up. "I can offer this one," he said.

"The Broker packed his pipe for a smoke,
But he found that his lighter was broke.
    He cried in despair;
    His grief rent the air,
Till a Snark lit him up with a stroke."

The Banker stood back up. Everyone was expecting another limerick, but instead he said, "I'd like to nominate Marcus Bernstein to be the Butcher. He may not have a pet Boojum Tree, but he does know everything that's printable about Henry Holiday, and he's presently writing a very boring biography of him. He has a beautifully framed map that is a perfect and absolute blank hung in the kitchen over his breakfast table. He has a collection of fossilized teeth, which he swears proves the existence of the Bandersnatch. Like any self-respecting butcher, he's a carnivore. In short, he'd be a perfect Butcher."

Again there was a round of applause and laughter

"Are there any further nominations?" the Bellman asked. He waited a moment, but none were forthcoming.

"Very well. Since there is only one nomination for the Butcher, we shall invite Marcus Bernstein to join us in that role. For the position of Beaver, we will cast secret ballots." Before passing out small strips of paper and pencils for the crew to mark their choice, he recited:

"The method employed I would gladly explain,
   While I have it so clear in my head,
If I had but the time and you had but the brain—
   But much yet remains to be said."

Everyone laughed. "Please mark your ballots and pass them up to me. We would normally have the Beaver and Butcher tally the votes and check the sums, but they are, after all, sadly departed, and in fact the very reason for this election." He tingled his bell three times in their memory.

The crewmen voted, and passed their ballots to the Captain. "There are five votes for Dr. Kerr and only two for Wanda Kerley," he announced after he had counted them. "Obviously not all of you are fond of cheesecake! Since there was not a tie I will not cast a vote. We will invite Marcus Bernstein to join us. In the unlikely event that he declines we will invite Wanda Kerley." He tingled his bell three times. "What I tell you three times is true," he said, and repeated the results of the vote two more times to make it official, as required by the Club's bylaws.

Having finished the business portion of the meeting, which they tried to limit severely as a matter of principle, it was time for reading the poem. This privilege passed from crewmember to crewmember on a simple rotation basis. It was to have been the Beaver's turn, but since no one present knew how to channel her this passed automatically to the Broker. He stood up and read the poem from beginning to end with great emotion. When he had finished they applauded, and had another cognac.

A keepsake was produced for each meeting, strictly limited to an edition of ten copies. This keepsake was typically a printing of a quote from or a specially commissioned illustration for *The Snark*. The only legal way to obtain any of these keepsakes was to be a member of the club or to inherit them from a member, since the crewmen were sworn to never place them on sale unless the club was disbanded, which no one could envision ever happening. Responsibility for producing the keepsake was also rotated through the crew, and each member strove to produce something of lasting beauty.

The keepsake for the evening was the Baker's responsibility, and Julia Castor stood up to make the presentation to the crew. She had brought only seven copies, having left her own at home and destroyed the copies that would have been given to the Butcher and Beaver. She passed them round like the Bellman serving out grog. The keepsake was a small cardboard mechanical device, printed in full colour and manufactured by hand by a craftsman in Venice. It showed the Baker perched on top of a crag, wildly waving his arms. A message in a small, framed window at the bottom said, "'It's a Snark!" When the scene was rotated by means of a wheel, the Baker rotated with it and softly and silently vanished, while the message in the framed window at the bottom simultaneously changed to, "It's a Boo—"

Everyone seemed to be thrilled with the keepsake, and they gave Julia a round of applause. She beamed in their approval. It was late and the crewmen said their good-byes and most retired to their rooms. A few went down to the bar for more grog.

Julia entered her room and took off her shoes, which were killing her. She was sure that she smelled like cigars and decided to take a shower and wash her hair before going to bed. As she was searching through her suitcase for a nightgown she failed to see a figure dressed entirely in black slip out from behind the curtains and approach her from behind. The killer stabbed her viciously in her left kidney and the pain was so severe that she could not even cry out. She crumpled to the floor. Her assailant calmly left the room, dropping the knife in plain view. Julia managed to crawl to the bedside phone and call the front desk, but bled to death before Security arrived.

Fit VI
Valentine's Day

Valentine's Day

$\mathcal{N}$ ews of Julia Castor's murder screamed across the nation's headlines like the voice of a Jubjub. Pinkman first heard the shrill news on CNN when he got out of bed to go to work. He picked up a copy of the Fresno newspaper and a cup of coffee at a GO Mart on the way to the Station. He read the front-page article as he sat behind his car in the parking lot, drinking his java.

"BOOJUM SNARK" STRIKES AGAIN AT DEL CORONADO
Woman Stabbed in the Back after Attending Secret "Snark Club" Meeting
San Diego (UPI) - SDPD report the murder of Los Angeles attorney Julia Castor. She was discovered dead in her hotel room late last night by hotel security at the historic Hotel del Coronado, in the same room once used by Tony Curtis during the filming of *Some Like it Hot*.

She had been stabbed in the back on returning to her room after attending a meeting of the secretive 'Snark Club', of which she was a long-time member.

SDPD homicide detectives and FBI agents are continuing to interview the remaining seven members of the club who were in attendance. All are citizens of Los Angeles and members of the American Lewis Carroll Society (ALCS).

The FBI has confirmed that the killer left a message, which is a quote from Lewis Carroll's now-infamous nonsense poem, *The Hunting of the Snark*. This links the Castor murder to three other attacks earlier this year, two of which were also fatal.

Fresno resident Fred Poole narrowly survived a letter bomb, while Alison Cooksley, also of Fresno, died in her shower from a bomb hidden in a free sample bottle of shampoo. George Clapham of Los Angeles was murdered with a shovel.

UPI contacted Dr. Grant Kerr, President of the California Chapter of the ALCS, to find out more about The Snark Club. "I've heard rumours of The Snark Club's existence for many years, but I'd never seen any real proof. Until last night's murder I had no idea what they did, or when or where they met." When asked why the club would be secret he said, "I can't imagine."

All of the club's members are also members of the California Chapter of the ALCS. The Snark Club's President, Roger Bellamy, held a press conference this morning to vigorously deny rumours of orgies and Satanic worship at the Snark Club's past meetings.

Other members of the once-secret Snark Club are: K. Biswas, J. Imhoff, J. Moldenhauer, R. Loder, D. Hink, and P. Gent.

LAPD, SDPD, ATF, and FBI all seemed to be completely 'snarked" by the case, and are appealing to the public to come forward if they have any information that might help lead to the arrest of the killer.

The Justice Department has offered a $1 million reward for information leading to the killer's arrest and conviction.

Pinkman finished his coffee and drove to work. His partner was already there, reading the newspaper that Detective Cox had given him. "You see this?" Jinks asked Pinkman, holding up the newspaper.

"Yes. I picked up a copy from a newsstand. Have you requested a copy of the San Diego case report?"

"Yes. I'm expecting it over the fax any minute."

Pinkman glanced at his desk and noticed that someone had placed a thimble on it. "Did you get a thimble, too?" he asked Jinks.

"No, they left me a bar of soap." He held it up. It was from The Holiday Inn.

Just then they heard the fax and Jinks retrieved the report. He read the highlights aloud. "She bled to death from a stab wound to the left kidney. The murder weapon, a fish filleting knife with a thin blade, was dropped at the scene and recovered. There were no fingerprints. The engraved message on a strip of stainless steel reads: 'A second-hand dagger-proof coat.'"

"Big surprise!" Pinkman said, interrupting him.

"The silly Snark Club appears to be innocent. Ten people meet once a year for seafood, cognac and illegal Cuban cigars, then read the poem to each other. Each member is named after a crewmember in the poem. Julia Castor was the Baker."

"These people are nuts!"

"I suppose they must just like each other and use it as an excuse to get together. I can't see that it's any worse than a ball game and pizza afterwards."

"No, I suppose not. But when people go to a ball game they don't usually end up knifing each other."

"Not usually; but it happens. Anyway, there's nothing here to indicate the killer was a member of the Club. However, half of their alibis can't be verified, since they said they simply went to bed. They were all staying at the hotel for the evening, since they tend to drink heavily at their meetings. There's a list in the case report of names of all of the members and their honorary Club titles. I did a comparison with our own list and there are significant differences. Here take a look." Jinks handed Pinkman a sheet of paper. "I put an 'X' by the victims. Poole is the only one not on both lists. I also listed Dr. Kerr, since we agreed that he is a suspect."

Crewman	Suspect List	Snark Club
Baker	Cooksley ×	Castor ×
Boots	Schwartz	Moldenhauer
Bonnets	Barnett	Loder
Beaver	Castor ×	Clapham ×
Broker	Imhoff	Imhoff
Billiard	Poole ×	Hink
Bellman	Clapham ×	Bellamy
Banker	Trocan	Biswas
Barrister	Jurist	Gant
Butcher	Cleaver	Cooksley ×
	Kerr	

"I suppose there's no reason why the lists should be identical. Perhaps all this tells us is that the killer might not be a member of The Snark Club. If he was just killing off members of the Club then why would Poole have been his first victim?"

"Makes sense. Okay, if that's true then we can probably take Imhoff off our list of suspects. He's the only one on both lists."

"I forgot to tell you. Zabrodski's coming in to see us again."

He had no sooner said this than Zabrodski walked in. "Can I talk with you two somewhere in private?"

"Sure," Pinkman said, and got up to lead the way to an empty interrogation room.

"I assume that you've seen the list of members of The Snark Club?" Zabrodski asked.

Pinkman and Jinks nodded.

"You know anything about them that we should know?"

"I can't think of anything. I assume you and the FBI are doing background checks on all of them."

"Yeah, that in progress. It will be a few weeks before they're complete."

"I'd suggest that you put Schwartz, Barnett, Imhoff, Trocan, Jurist, Cleaver, and Kerr under surveillance or provide protection," Pinkman said. "In our opinion one of them is highly likely to be the next victim."

"You have any basis for that?"

"Just our old list, which you"ve seen. So far all four victims were on the list. I'd bet serious money that the next one will be too."

"Let me know if you find out anything which might indicate which one is most likely, will you?" He had begun to daydream about the huge reward for finding the killer and how he would spend it; and it wouldn't be on old books, either.

"Will do," Pinkman assured him, though he didn't really mean it. He didn't want to share a million-dollar reward with anyone other than Jinks.

Agent Zabrodski left.

"Who do you think the next victim will be? You got any hunches?" Pinkman asked Jinks.

"I'd guess Schwartz, just because the Boots is the second crewman mentioned in the poem. He's already killed the first one."

"That's as good as any, I suppose. It's too bad we don't have the resources to put round-the-clock surveillance on her."

"Yeah, it might save her life."

Babs was seated on one of the couches in the living room, reading Lynne Truss's *Tennyson's Gift*. Every few minutes she would laugh hysterically. "This is the funniest book I've ever read!" she told Grant as he walked in carrying two packages, one very large one, and the other large enough for a sweater.

"You just like it because it's so hard on Dodgson," Grant said. "I didn't find it nearly so amusing."

"You wouldn't. That's because you idolize him," she said. "He's like a god to you."

"He's not a god to me," Grant objected. "Just because I like and collect his books doesn't mean that I worship him."

"Of course you do. You built that enormous shrine to him in there," she said, pointing to the library, "and you've filled it with his holy scriptures. You have more of his *Wonderland Bibles* in there than the Gideons have the real thing in hotel rooms. Every day you go in there and sacrifice your time and money, like a priest."

"That's a bit harsh!"

"Harsh? You even helped found the California mission for the mother church, the American Lewis Carroll Society! You've made hundreds of converts."

He decided to try to change the subject. "It's Valentine's Day," he said, giving her as warm a smile as he could after her abuse.

"I know."

"I have some presents."

"Why? Do you want me to be your little valentine, Grant?"

"Well, yes, I guess you could put it that way. After all, we are married." He moved the large, heavy package over to her with some effort. It was wrapped in a bright red foil and tied with a white ribbon. He propped up the package while she unwrapped it.

"It's gorgeous!" she said, with sincerity. He smiled broadly. He knew she would like it.

"Who is the calligrapher?" she asked.

"Hiro Yoshizawa."

"When was it done?"

"Sometime in the seventeenth century. The date's a little uncertain."

"Do you know the translation?"

"Not accurately. It's very stylized and difficult to decipher. They told me that the only words that are recognizable with certainty are 'plum', 'lips' and 'moon'. I guess you'll have to make up your own poem that includes those words."

"Thank you, Grant. It's very beautiful."

"You're welcome," he said, then sat there looking at her as if he expected her to give him something.

"What is it grant?"

"Well, I was sort of hoping that you might have a little something for me," he said, expecting her to produce the book he had discovered in her lingerie drawer.

"Why would you think that?" she said. "Frankly, I wasn't expecting anything from you, and I didn't get anything for you. Sorry, Grant. I didn't think you knew I existed."

Grant gave her a puzzled, hurt look.

It suddenly clicked in Babs' mind that it had been Grant messing around in her lingerie. "He's found the *Snark* and thinks it's a present for him!" she thought. "I wonder if he's looked at it!" She decided to change the subject.

"What's in the other package, Grant?"

He hesitated, then handed it to her without saying anything.

She opened it and pulled out a very scanty two-piece pink leather and chains outfit. "You've got to be kidding!" she said.

"Why?" He was very disappointed by the tone of her voice. "You would be beautiful in it."

"There's no way I'm putting that thing on!" she said with finality and tossed it and the box in his lap. She got up and stomped towards the hallway, leaving Grant sitting on the couch with his mouth open and propping up the calligraphy. The lingerie fell on the carpet. "Find yourself a whore if you like that sort of thing!" she snarled at him as she went through the door towards her frigid suite. She locked the door and went straight to the closet to retrieve the book. She wasn't sure if he had looked at the first chapter or not, and there was no way to know. She put on latex gloves and tore out the first chapter, then stuffed it into a large handbag. She got in her Alpha Romeo and drove to a seedy part of town, then up and down a few alleys until she found an appropriate dumpster. She drove up next to it and tossed the handbag with the Snark chapter into it, then drove away.

She hadn't noticed Nizar Gulam, watching her from behind another dumpster. Nizar was always interested in anything anyone threw away, since this was basically how he made a living, such as it was. It struck him very odd that an attractive, well-dressed woman, driving an Alpha Romeo, would throw a handbag into a dumpster. He noted her license plate number, and scratched it on the side of the dumpster with a pocketknife, so he wouldn't forget it. If she was throwing away stolen property there might be a reward for information. When she had turned at the street and was out of sight he scrambled into the dumpster and retrieved the handbag.

He opened the handbag and pulled out the folded chapter, took a quick look and dropped it to the pavement. He then went through the bag carefully, looking for money or drugs. There was nothing. He ripped out the lining, but still found nothing. In frustration he threw the handbag back into the dumpster and walked away. However, after he'd gone a short distance he decided that perhaps he should take a closer look at the paper. He went back and opened it out onto the filthy paving. He read the first verse slowly, struggling with the words, and saying them aloud: *"Just the place for a Snark! the Bellman cried as he landed his crew with care; supporting each man on the top of the tide by a finger entwined in his hair."* He paused after the struggle. "Sounds like nonsense!" he said, which of course it was, and gave up trying to read it, since it just wasn't worth the effort. He folded it back up and stuffed it inside the plastic bag he always carried with him for empty aluminium cans.

Fit VII
The Hunting

The Hunting

*G*rant drove downtown to the Farrell Building, an ugly 1950s office tower with twenty-three floors, of which about half were empty and for lease. People weren't exactly lined up wanting to move in. He parked his BMW across the street in a high-priced parking structure, hoping that it would be less likely to be stolen or stripped. He took the elevator to the tenth floor where a private investigator named Świątkiewicz had a small office. The PI shared the floor with a number of small businesses, including a not very successful dentist, a starving lawyer and a Korean urologist. The hallway was hot and stuffy and smelled like garlic.

He found Świątkiewicz's office and went in without knocking. The office was bleakly furnished with three worn-out upholstered chairs that looked like dentist office rejects, an end table with a ugly lamp, and a stack of old *Sports Illustrated* magazines. An attractive young receptionist sat behind an old grey metal desk, reading a Harlequin romance. There was a cheap tan four-drawer filing cabinet with a large dent in the top drawer behind her, and a PC on her otherwise empty desk.

She put down her paperback and smiled at Grant. "May I help you?"

"I have an appointment. My name is Dr. Grant Kerr."

"Oh, yes! Mr. Swat is expecting you."

"Mr. Swat?"

"Oh, that's what everyone calls him. No one except his family and ex-wife can pronounce his name, and the ex-wife usually refers to him as something much ruder."

Grant smiled. "You're sure he won't mind me calling him Swat?"

"I'm sure of it! That's what they called him when he played football. Just a moment; I'll tell him you're here." She got up and went into an inside office, then reappeared momentarily. "He'll see you now, Dr. Kerr."

Grant went in. Swat stood up then shook Grant's hand over the top of his bare desk. "He's either very neat or needs work," Grant thought.

"Pecheniuk Świątkiewicz," he said; "but you can call me Swat if you like. I realize that practically no one in this country can pronounce my name, much less spell it." Swat had played for the Rams for two years as a defensive lineman before he tore up his knee; he was a very large man, and still in formidable shape. He was dressed in dark slacks and a cream coloured Polo shirt, and looked more like a bouncer than a detective.

"It's nice to meet you. Your receptionist had already mentioned that I should call you Swat."

"Good. What can I do for you, Mr. Kerr?"

"I assume that you've heard about the so-called "Boojum" Snark murders?"

"Of course; it's been in the news for months. I'm all read up on them."

"I'm President of the California Chapter of the American Lewis Carroll Society. All of the victims have been members of our Society. We're concerned that more of our members may also be targets of this psychopath. We need to do everything we can to stop him. "

"I understand that there's a task force of about a hundred officers from a dozen police forces and Federal agencies trying to do just that," Swat said.

"Trying is the operative word. So far they have been completely ineffectual. Our members are quitting out of fear."

"Can't say that I blame any of them," Swat allowed.

"No; you're quite right. At this rate we will soon cease to exist. And I'm getting a bit nervous myself. All of those who have been attacked have been collectors of Carroll's *The Hunting of the Snark*. My own collection is probably larger than all of theirs put together. Actually, I'm surprised I wasn't his first victim."

"Why do you say 'his'?" Swat asked. "Are you certain it's a man?"

"Well, no. I just assumed that it was. After all, the murders have been bombings and assaults. You don't normally think of a woman being capable of doing such things."

"A woman shot Linen in the head at close range," Swat said.

"Really? I had never heard that. I see what you mean."

"What do you think that I might do that the police aren't already doing?"

"I'm not sure, exactly. Perhaps there's some rumour on the street. The bomber had to get explosives from somewhere. Perhaps you could find out from whom. Perhaps there is an accomplice. I'd just like for you to snoop around; see if you can come up with anything. "

"Do you want a body guard?"

"I hadn't really considered that, but I suppose that might be a wise precaution."

"My fee is $400 a day plus expenses if the job takes me out of town. I can drive you around, stay with you at work, and even live in your home if you want. Or I can just stake out your house and watch for anything suspicious. If there is someone that you suspect might be the killer I can try to find him or her and watch where they go and what they do."

"I don't have any suspects in mind. I can't imagine who could be doing these things."

"Do you want a body guard?" he asked again.

"Yes; that would be smart, I think. When could you start that?"

"Tonight. I could drop by about 7:00. I'll need your address and phone number."

"Okay." Grant took out a business card and handed it to him. "We live in Brentwood."

"I know the area. I'll be there. You might warn your wife, if you have one. I wouldn't want to scare her by showing up unannounced."

"Right; I'll do that. Thank you. See you this evening."

Swat nodded, and shook Grant's hand. "Please leave a check for $5,000 as a retainer with Mary Anne as you leave."

Grant nodded and went back out to the reception area, where wrote out the check. He felt a bit better.

When he went to collect his car he found that his transmission had been stolen.

When he complained to the attendant, a balding Chinese man with bad teeth, he shrugged his shoulders and pointed to a sign, saying, "No responsible for stolen! You pay $7 parking! You no pay, I call police!"

Grant paid him, then used his cell phone to call for a wrecker and a cab.

When Grant finally got home later that evening, driving a rental car, he went looking for Babs to tell her that Swat would be arriving that evening. She was locked in her icebox.

"Babs?" he yelled through the door.

"Go away!" she yelled back at him.

He knew better than to argue when she had that bitchy tone of voice, and went to the library. If Swat scared her, too bad; he'd tried.

An hour later Babs came out of her suite and went down to the library to see if Grant was still there. She peeked in the door and saw him typing away at the PC in the dim light. She pulled on a pair of latex gloves and eased the door closed. She locked it with her key, then went down the hallway and unlocked the closet where the alarm system control panel was located. She punched in the passkey to activate the fire suppression system and manually triggered it.

A shrill alarm went off immediately and she went back to her suite and locked herself in. She took several strong sedatives and crawled into bed. When the firemen arrived she wanted to be sure that they found her asleep.

Inside the library Grant reacted immediately to the alarm, realizing that he only had seconds to respond. He jerked open the bottom drawer of his desk and pulled out a small fresh air mask with an attached compressed air cylinder and managed to put it on just as the Halon system activated and began flooding the room. He had fifteen minutes capacity on the mask.

He rushed to the door and found it locked. He momentarily panicked, then remembered the spare key he had in his desk. He retrieved it and escaped into the hallway, then closed and locked the door behind him to prevent Halon from flooding the rest of the house or anyone going in, which might be fatal. He took off the mask and went outside to wait at the front door for the fire trucks to arrive.

Two trucks and a rescue van arrived about ten minutes later with lights on, and horns and sirens blaring. He explained that the system had been accidentally tripped and that there was in fact no fire. They wanted to go inside and check until he explained that the Halon system had flooded the library and it was too hazardous to enter the room. They left and he went back inside to start the ventilation system that would clear out the Halon.

Grant went to Bab's suite to check on her. When she didn't respond to his knocks he let himself in using his master key. He found her sound asleep, and he left her alone. It never occurred to him that she had tried to kill him.

* * * *
* * *
* * * *

A few days after Nizar Gulam found the incriminating chapter in the dumpster he came across a used bookstore on his daily rounds of searching for aluminium cans. In spite of its pretentious name, Catcher in the Rye Antiquarian Books was nothing more than a junk bookstore, specializing in paperbacks and abused girlie magazines. The owner, Rodeny Bryer, had chosen the name because *Catcher in the Rye* was the only piece of genuine literature that he'd ever read from cover to cover. The shop's walls were lined with shelves knocked together from 1x12 lumber, filled with well-read and dog-eared romance, mystery and sci-fi novels, and a few Penguins and other mass market classics. The only antiquarian book in the shop was an old worn-out copy of *The Wizard of Oz*, which Rodney imagined to be worth hundreds of dollars. Nizar went in and looked around. The old books smelled almost as bad as he did. The only customer in the shop was a balding man who looked to be in his sixties. He was wearing an old flannel shirt and baggy pants, and was flipping quickly through an old *Playboy*. Nizar went up to the counter.

"What do you want?" snarled Rodney. He was smoking and the effort of talking caused him to cough violently, as if trying to expectorate a piece of his lung. Rodney didn't like street people coming into his shop, since they invariably wanted a hand-out and never bought anything.

Nizar dug around beneath the cans in his plastic bag until he found the folded chapter. "You interested in this?" he asked hopefully, placing it on the counter. It had become rather heavily stained and damp from the cola and beer that had leaked from some of the cans.

Rodney opened it up with the end of a pencil, as carefully as he might poke at a landmine, not wanting to touch the filthy thing. He recognized the poem, though he had never seen this particular set of illustrations. "It's from *The Hunting of the Snark*," he said. "It's a children's book for adults. I think Lewis Carroll wrote it; or maybe it was Edward Lear; I can't really remember. Why'd you rip out of the book and mark all over it? It's nothing but a piece of garbage now!"

Nizar wasn't encouraged by this assessment. "I didn't rip it out or mark it up. That's how I found it."

"Where'd you find it?"

"In a dumpster. I figured it might be worth something."

"Not to me."

"Not even five bucks?"

"You've got to be kidding!"

Nizar put it back into his plastic trash bag, and then turned to leave. The old guy looking at the *Playboy* made a strange noise and both Rodney and Nizar turned to look at him, half expecting to see him collapse from a heart attack.

Suddenly Rodney's neurons fired and he recalled reading about the Boojum Snark murders. He also remembered that there was a huge reward involved for information leading to an arrest and conviction, though he couldn't recall the exact amount. "Hey!" he yelled.

The customer in the back froze, as if he had been caught ripping out the centrefold, and Nizar stopped with his hand on the doorknob. Nizar asked, "Me"

"Yeah, you. Come back here a minute." Rodney motioned to him.

Nizar walked back to the counter and the customer resumed his furtive thumbing. "Yeah?"

"Tell you what; there's a woman comes in here sometimes looking for Lewis Carroll stuff. She might be interested in that piece of garbage. I'll give you a buck for it on a gamble that I can sell it to her. That's the best I can do."

Nizar hesitated. He had hoped for much more. Still, a dollar was better than nothing. He pulled it back out of the bag and handed it to him across the counter.

When he had gone, Rodney called the FBI. After several transfers he connected to the agent in charge of the case. "Arnold Schlichenmayer. May I help you?"

"I understand there's a reward for information leading to the arrest and conviction of the Snark bomber," Rodney said. The customer in the back stopped looking at the magazine when he heard this and Rodney noticed.

"Just a minute," Rodney told Schlichenmayer; "I got to deal with a customer. "Hey you! Since you ain't buyin' nothin, get your butt outta here!" The old man frowned, crammed the magazine back onto a self and shuffled out with a glare. "Sorry about that," he said into the phone. "Guys come in here and act like it's a damn public library. I'm goin' to have to start bagging things up in plastic. As I was askin', is there a reward?"

"Yes. The Justice Department is offering a reward of one-million dollars."

This was bigger than he had remembered. "I may have something for you."

"What is it?"

"It's a chapter torn out of a copy of *The Hunting of the Snark*. It's got names written across the faces of the characters in the poem. Four of them are victims."

"How do you know?"

"I checked their names against a newspaper article; it's public knowledge."

"Can you bring it in?"

"No. I run a bookshop. I don't have anyone to watch it for me."

"What's your name and address? I'll drop by and see you this afternoon."

"Rodney Bryer. My shop's called Catcher in the Rye Antiquarian Books." He gave him the address.

"Please don't handle the paper; there may be fingerprints of interest on it. Place it in a plastic bag and keep it in a safe place until I get there."

"Okay. When will you be by?"

"Within the hour. Thank you for calling."

"Right."

They rang off.

Schlichenmayer picked up a technician on his way out, and they rushed over to Catcher in the Rye Antiquarian Books. They went in and identified themselves. "Let's see what you've got," he told Rodney.

Rodney pulled a plastic bag out from under the counter and handed it to him.

The technician put on gloves and opened it up. They looked it over briefly and Schlichenmayer said, "Bag it up," at which the technician took a large plastic Ziploc bag out of a small case he had brought with him and inserted it. He then labelled it with a marker.

Schlichenmayer wrote out a receipt and handed it to Rodney. "We need your fingerprints," he said; "so we can figure out which fingerprints on that paper are yours. You ever been fingerprinted?"

"Yeah. A few times. "

"By whom?"

"LAPD."

"Okay. We can get them from there. No need to get a new set from you. Do you have any outstanding warrants?"

"I don't know; maybe a traffic warrant. Why?"

"I'd go take care of that if I were you. You may end up in the limelight if this is significant. You could find yourself in jail."

"Yeah. Okay, I'll do that."

"Where did you get this?"

"A guy came in off the street and offered it to me for five bucks. I gave him a dollar. Just remember that it's my property now."

"If it's what it looks like you won't be seeing it again, since it will go into evidence. If you're lucky, there may be a chunk of the reward coming to you. If it turns out to be nothing we will return it to you."

"What do you mean by "a chunk" of the reward? Why wouldn't I get all of it?"

"You might. But then maybe the guy who found it might get some of that reward as well. A judge would have to decide. Do you know this street person's name?"

"No idea. I never saw him before he came in here today."

"Can you describe him?"

"Dirty and smelly."

"That describes at least a third of L. A. What else?"

"Thirtyish; shoulder length black hair, with some grey in it. He's shorter than me. Rough looking, from living on the street; gaunt. No beard, but not clean-shaven either. He was wearing an old Raiders tee shirt, jeans and sneakers."

"Any distinguishing marks? Tattoos? That sort of thing. "

Rodney thought for a moment. "You mean other than the fact that he's blind in one eye?"

Schlichenmayer rolled his eyes. "Now, don't you think that it might be of some importance when describing someone to say that he was blind in one eye? What else? Did he have both of his hands and feet?"

Rodney was offended. "Yeah, he had both hands and feet."

"Both ears?"

"Yeah."

"Schlichenmayer handed him a card with his phone number. "Call me if you see him again. Try to get a name if you can." Rodney took the card and studied it.

"Okay, but I doubt I'll see him. He doesn't look like the type that reads a lot."

"Oh, I don't know; he obviously collects Victorian poetry." They turned to leave. "We'll be in touch."

They left.

Rodney started thinking about having to share the million dollar reward with some street person, and decided that he didn't much like that idea. He put the pistol he kept under the counter in his jacket pocket, closed his shop and went looking for him. He figured he had to be within walking distance, though that might still be a rather large area.

Fit VIII
The Vanishing

The Vanishing

*B*abs woke up about four hours after the incident in the library, still groggy from the sedative. She lay there for another fifteen minutes until her mind began to clear. She got up and washed her face with cold water, then went out into the hallway and down to the library, which was empty. She went into the living room looking for Grant and was startled to find Swat sitting on one of the sofas, watching TV.

He stood up when he heard her come in. "Who the hell are you?" she demanded.

"Pecheniuk Świątkiewicz. I'm a private investigator. Your husband hired me today to look after him."

"Where is he?"

"He went to the kitchen for a beer."

Grant walked in, interrupting their conversation. "Oh, you're awake!" he said to her. "You missed all of the excitement."

"What excitement?"

"Someone tried to kill me a few hours ago."

"They did what!"

"Tried to kill me. Locked the door to the library and tripped the fire suppression system."

"How did you escape? Did Arnold Schwarzenegger here help you?"

"It's Pecheniuk Świątkiewicz," the PI corrected her.

"Whatever," she said. "I'll just yell, 'Arnold,' if I need you; which I don't foresee."

"Swat wasn't here yet," Grant explained.

"Squat?" she said.

"Not 'Squat'; it's 'Swat'. It's Mr. Świątkiewicz's nickname."

"As in SWAT Team?"

"I suppose. Actually, as it happened, I was able to save myself. I had taken the precaution of placing a fresh air mask in the bottom desk drawer. When I heard the alarm go off I put it on. Luckily, I also had a spare key in the desk, so 1 was able to let myself out."

"Why would anyone want to kill you?"

"For the same reason the Snark's been killing the others, I suppose."

"Is Arnold here spending the night? I need to know whether to lock my door at night." She glared at Swat, who just stood there impassive and impervious to her insults. After several years in the NFL trenches he didn't intimidate easily.

"Yes, he'll be staying here for a while. After the incident this afternoon I don't want him too far away."

"How was the killer able to trip the system?" she asked.

"That's an interesting question, Babs. The police wanted to know the same thing. They were here earlier, and said that it had to be someone who knew the passkey number. That narrows it down a bit."

"Not really," she said. "It's written down on a piece of paper stuck on the refrigerator door with a magnet. Anyone who's been in the kitchen over the past few months could have seen it."

"You have it posted on the refrigerator?" Grant asked in shocked disbelief.

"Just in case I forget it."

Grant shook his head. "Millions of dollars' worth of books in there, guarded by a sophisticated alarm system, and you put the passkey number on the fridge?"

She shrugged. "Well, excuuuuse me!"

"It's okay, Babs; don't get upset! We can reset the alarm to a new number. But please, don't post it in plain view!"

"Why didn't you wake me when all of this was going on?" she demanded.

"I tried to, but you were out cold. I couldn't rouse you. Everything was all right, so I just let you sleep."

"I may have overdone it with the sedative," she said. "I had a bad headache and wanted to go right to sleep. Well, I'm glad you're okay," she lied. "I'm going out for sushi. I'm hungry." She turned and left the room for her suite.

Grant turned to Swat and said, "She's a pistol!"

"I can see that. Strange; she didn't seem all that upset, though. Most wives would have been all over you, patting your hand and carrying on."

"Not Babs; not her style."

Schlichenmayer received the lab report on the torn out chapter provided by Rodney Bryer several days later. They had identified the chapter as having been from the Catalpa Press, London edition of *The Hunting of the Snark*. There were quite a number of fingerprints. The book had been well read. The only prints that were identifiable were Rodney Bryer's and those belonging to a petty criminal named Nizar Gulam who was homeless and living somewhere in L.A. Mug shots taken by LAPD following his previous arrests were attached. Gulam's lengthy rap sheet was also attached; it was primarily for vagrancy, shoplifting and petty theft; he had spent time in the L. A. County Jail on several occasions. Stains on the paper were identified as Pepsi Cola, beer and dog urine; there were no detectable human bodily fluids. Marks-A-Lot felt pens had been used to write names across the faces, and all of these names were also listed on the membership rolls of both the American Lewis Carroll Society and its California Chapter. They included all of the known victims of the so-called "Boojum" Snark killer.

Schlichenmayer issued an arrest warrant for Nizar Gulam and sent copies to all agencies and police departments working on the case. His old mug shots were distributed to local new organizations and would be on the front page of local and many national newspapers and TV newscasts the next day, along with cautionary notes that he should be considered armed and extremely dangerous.

Świątkiewicz was one of many people in L. A. who recognized him immediately when they saw his face broadcast on the local nightly news. Swat got in his car and raced downtown to prowl the alleys and see if he could find him before the FBI, LAPD or someone else picked him up. There was a million-dollar reward involved and Swat wanted to find out what Nizar knew about the murders before the police did.

It took him less than an hour to find him, crouched behind a dumpster eating the remains of someone's Chinese dinner out of a Styrofoam container.

"You're in big trouble, Nizar," he said as he reached down and easily lifted him into an upright position. Nizar dropped the remains of the beef in black bean sauce.

"Swat!" he said, recognizing him from a few unpleasant past encounters. "Why's that? I ain't done nothin'!"

"That's not what the FBI thinks. You ought to read the papers once in a while. Your ugly mug's on the front page of practically every newspaper in the country; you've even made CNN."

"Why?" he asked, completely dumbfounded.

"For some reason they seem to think you're the "Boojum" Snark serial killer."

"Who? Me?"

"Yeah, you."

"I've never killed nothin' in my life!" he protested.

"Yeah, I know. And you don't have the brains or the strength, either."

"Why would they think I'm the serial killer?"

"I haven't any idea," he said truthfully. "We're going for a little ride, Nizar," he continued, then picked him up as easily as he would a child and carried him to his car. He stuffed him into the passenger seat, and buckled him in. "You try to get out and I'll break your back," he said with genuine menace.

Nizar believed him, and wasn't about to try anything that foolish.

"Every cop in L. A. is out scouring around in alleys and under rocks looking for you. We need somewhere a little more private to try and jog your memory."

Swat drove to the top level of a multi-level car park. It was empty since no one wanted the sun to fade the paint on his car.

"Now you need to start thinking real hard," Swat said. "What do you know about snarks?"

"What's a snark?"

"Oh, it's a scary little monster in a fairy tale."

"I don't read fairy tales."

"I'm sure you don't read much of anything." He reached over and took Nizar's left hand, then casually broke his index finger, as easily as snapping a pencil. Nizar screamed in agony at the worst pain he had ever felt in his life. Swat looked at him as murderously as a Bandersnatch contemplating a Banker for dinner. "Your memory any better yet?" he asked.

Nizar shook his head, tears and snot streaming down his face. He gingerly held his left hand with his right, and rocked back and forth on the car seat in a vain effort to ease the throbbing pain in his already swollen finger.

"You got nine more fingers to help fix that lousy memory of yours."

Nizar screamed again, just at the thought. He started thinking desperately about anything that he had ever heard of snarks.

Swat reached over and took Nizar's right index finger, prepared to break it next.

"Wait!" Nizar screamed. "I just thought of something!"

"I'm waiting; but, as you know, I'm not a real patient man."

"I watched this lady throw a handbag into a dumpster about a week ago. I crawled into the dumpster and got it. All it had in it was some pages torn out of a book."

"What's that got to do with snarks?"

"I took it over to a used bookstore and sold it for a buck. The guy told me it was torn out of a book about hunting snarks."

"What did these pages look like?"

"It was real weird; all folded up, like an accordion. I stretched it out and it was maybe twenty feet long. There was this long, goofy-looking boat, with cartoons of men with big heads looking over the railing. Someone had wrote names across their faces with a marker. Some of them had a big X drawn across their face, too. And there was a long poem written down the whole thing. I read the first verse, but it sounded like some sort of nonsense, so I didn't bother to read the whole thing. I think I remember somethin' about a hotel bellman holding up some guy by his hair; somethin" stupid like that."

"Why would anyone give you a dollar for that?"

"The guy said he had a customer that liked this stuff and he thought he could sell it to her."

"The lady who threw it in the dumpster; what'd she look like?"

"She looked like a movie star. Dark brown hair. I didn't see her real good, though, 'cause she didn't get out of the car; she just threw it in the dumpster from her window."

"What was she driving?"

"A late model light blue Alpha Romeo; real nice."

"What's the license number?"

"I didn't notice," he lied and looked away.

Swat was still holding his right index finger. He broke it and Nizar screamed again, in excruciating pain. "Now, Nizar, you must think I'm real stupid. You think I'm stupid, Nizar?"

Nizar shook his head. "No; no. 1 know you ain't stupid."

"Now 1 know that if you saw something like that happen that you'd memorize that plate number; might be worth something. Right now it might be worth your life."

"I didn't memorize it. I scratched it on the side of the dumpster, 'cause I knew I'd forget it."

"Okay. We're going to go find it. You'd better hope someone hasn't taken that dumpster anywhere." He reached into his jacket and retrieved a set of handcuffs. He attached one to Nizar's left wrist and the other to an eyebolt that he had installed beneath the dash for such a purpose. "You do anything silly, like try to wave at a cop, and I'm going to put a bullet in your liver," he said. "No further warnings. Got it?" He opened his jacket so that Nizar could see the pistol he had in a shoulder holster.

"I'm not going to do anything like that," Nizar assured him, through teeth clenched in pain.

"I hope not, for your sake." He started the SUV and they drove out of the parking structure. Swat paid the attendant.

"Now exactly where is that dumpster you vandalized?" he said as he turned onto the street.

"I don't know the address. I'll just have to give you directions. Take a left at the next corner and then go about six blocks. Turn into the alley next to a Greek restaurant named Mykonos."

"I see your memory's improving. Who'd you sell the page to?"

"The owner of a bookshop called Catcher in the Rye Antiquarian Books. I don't know his name. He's a real jerk. I think he has lung cancer or TB; serves him right."

Swat turned in at the alley at the Mykonos restaurant.

"Stop here," Nizar said. "She threw it in that dumpster over there," he said, pointing with his chin. It hurt too much to point with his throbbing hands.

Swat got out and went around to the passenger side and uncuffed him. "Show me where you scratched the plate number."

Nizar led him to another dumpster about fifty feet away. "It's here," he said, pointing at it with his elbow, and grimacing from the pain caused by the movement.

Swat looked at it, and wrote it down. "Get back in the car."

Nizar reluctantly climbed back in. Swat buckled him back in and reattached the cuffs.

Swat took the freeways for over a hundred miles out into the desert towards Vegas, then turned north on a ranch road with a cattle guard. Nizar sat very still, trying not to move or bump his hands. He needed to urinate, but knew that he'd never be able to get his pants unzipped, so he decided to try and hold it. Eventually the pain in his bladder distracted him from the pain in his broken fingers. They drove another thirty miles, before turning up a dry arroyo, Swat driving the SUV on the hard creek bed. He stopped and got Nizar out. Nizar started to plead for his life, well aware that he was in a very serious situation. Swat ignored him and without so much as a goodbye, reached over and broke his skinny neck, as easily as one might wring the frail neck of a Jub-jub.

He removed the cuffs from Nizar's wrists and backed the SUV out to the road, then turned it around and parked it. He retrieved a Polaroid from the back seat and removed his boots. He cut off a sagebrush branch with a pocketknife, then hiked with the camera and branch to Nizar's body, where he took two photos of him. He then systematically obliterated the tire tracks and his own footprints, using the branch like a broom, walking backwards all the way back to the SUV. He got in and swept away his last footprints, closed the door and then drove away, tossing out the branch after he had gone another mile.

Once back in L. A., Swat stopped by his office and got on the Internet to track down the owner of the license plate. Just as he had expected, it was registered to Dr. Grant Kerr. Swat had seen Babs driving a blue Alpha Romeo and was sure it was her that Nizar had seen.

He went to a coin-operated car wash and methodically cleaned the SUV, including the undercarriage, wheel wells and other recesses where any dirt might have lodged. He wiped down the front seat and dash areas to remove any trace of fingerprints and bodily fluids such as tears or mucus and then vacuumed up every thread and hair. Satisfied that the car was clean enough to withstand a FBI search he went to a tire dealership and bought four new tires with a radically different tread pattern and had them mounted. He had them put the spares in the back, explaining that he wanted to keep them for off-roading. But, later that night he drove out Highway 1 until he was at an appropriate cliff and tossed the old tires into the ocean. He drove back to L. A. and went to a coin operated Laundromat where he washed all of his clothing with excess soap and very hot water, then dried them. He dropped them off in the first Salvation Army container he encountered, along with the shoes he had worn that day. Having finished his clean-up he drove to the Kerr's Brentwood mansion and rang the doorbell. Babs answered.

"Oh, it's you," she said, with as much disappointment in the tone of her voice as she could manage.

"Is the doctor in?" he asked.

"The doctor is definitely out," she said sarcastically.

"Good. It's you I wanted to talk to anyway." He pushed his way in and closed the door.

"About what?"

"The time has come, the Walrus said, to speak of many things," he said. "Of bombs, and death, and whether snarks have wings."

"What's that supposed to mean?" she snarled, not the least amused.

"I suppose you've seen the mug shots of a street person named Nizar Gulam. They've been on the front page and on TV. The FBI and LAPD have been searching for him. "

"Yes, I've seen them. What about them?"

"You might not be aware that Gulam witnessed you throw a handbag into a dumpster about a week ago. He had the good sense to write down your license plate number. He dug your bag out of the dumpster and inside it he found some pages that had been torn out of a copy of *The Hunting of the Snark*. He sold that to the owner of a second-hand bookstore, who in turn gave it to the FBI, hoping for the big reward that's been posted for information leading to the arrest and conviction of the same serial killer who tried to kill your husband in the library."

This was big news to Babs. She knew the police were searching for Gulam, but didn't know why, and was stunned to learn that the FBI now had the pages that she had tried to dispose of. "I knew I should have burned them," she thought, trying not to panic.

"And exactly who is this serial killer?" she asked, waiting to see if he really knew as much as he seemed to imply that he did.

"You're probably the only one who knows for sure. I figure that you're the killer. But another possibility is that you have an accomplice; perhaps a lover that you got to do it for you. Or even a hired killer; they're not hard to find in L. A."

"Why would I want to kill all of these people?"

"My guess is that you just got tired of your husband, and want his money. You've set out to kill him and throw suspicion on some mystical psychopath to cover your tracks."

"What do you want?" she asked.

"I can collect a million by turning you and Nizar over to the FBI. You'll go to prison. Now I realize that California doesn't like to execute women; but, at the very least, you'd spend the rest of your life waiting on death row. I think a better arrangement would be for you to give me two million instead."

"You would just continue to blackmail me, even if I agreed to the two million. After you spent that, you'd want another million, then another. And besides, Gulam could always turn me in."

"Here's my proposition. You give me the two million and I kill Nizar. I'll give you a photo to prove it and then tell the police where to find his body. You'll see it in the newspapers. They'll think he was the "Boojum" Snark killer and close the case. You'll have the photo of Nizar's body, with my fingerprints on it. If I ever try to blackmail you again you can turn that into the police and I'll go to death row for Nizar's murder, so I wouldn't dare. If you try to blackmail me to get your two million back I'll turn the tape recording of this conversation over to the police and give another copy to your husband. I would imagine that your husband would then either divorce you, or have you killed, even if the police don't do anything."

"What tape recording?,

He opened his jacket to reveal a pocketsize recorder, which was running. She glared at him.

"Deal?"

She thought for a moment, but couldn't see any way out of it. He was too big and strong to take the recording away from him, even if she did have a black belt in karate. He probably did too. "Deal," she finally said. "It will take a little while to get the money."

"How long? I'm not a patient man."

"Two full working days. I'll have to sell some stock."

"Okay. I want the money in old bills; nothing bigger than a hundred."

"It might take an extra day to come up with that many old bills."

"Okay, I'll give you three days." He opened the door and left.

"You might want to go out and buy yourself a second-hand dagger-proof coat," she said to him through the closed door.

Three days later Swat showed up at the Kerr mansion and rang the doorbell. Babs answered and let him in without saying anything, then closed it behind them.

"Do you have the photo?" she asked.

He didn't answer, but went in and searched the house to be sure there wasn't anyone hiding somewhere to eavesdrop. He came back to the foyer and took her by the wrist into a guest bathroom and turned on the faucets, just in case she had hidden a micro-cam or a tape recorder somewhere.

"Where's the money?"

"In my suite. I'll go and get it."

"I'll go with you," he said and pulled out his pistol, which he pointed at her. He followed her into her suite and into one of her huge walk-in closets.

"It's like the damn North Pole in here!" he remarked, glad that he'd worn a jacket. "No wonder you've got such a cold heart!"

She ignored him and bent down and opened an aluminium case sitting on the floor. "There's a million in used bills."

"What are you talking about? The deal was two million!"

"I'll give you the other million when I have proof that Gulam is dead."

He reached into a coat pocket and produced the Polaroid of Nizar, which he handed to her.

She stared at the photo. "This doesn't prove anything. You two could have faked this."

"You'll know tomorrow, when you see the newspaper headlines."

"Okay. Come back at 9:00 a.m. Grant will be gone to the office. If everything is as you say I'll give you the other million."

He picked up the suitcase and turned to leave. "9:00 a.m. sharp. If there's anything funny happening I'll kill you."

"I'm not a fool; everything will be in order. I already have the money; it's just in a safe place."

He motioned to her with his pistol for her to lead the way out of the house. She shut and locked the door after him.

Babs put the photo in an envelope and went immediately to a small bank in Orange, where she had a safe deposit box that only she knew about, and put it in the box.

She was up early the next morning to look at the newspaper.

"BOOJUM" SNARK SERIAL KILLER'S BODY FOUND IN NEVADA DESERT
Well Known Street-Person Nizar Gulam Dead from Broken Neck

Los Angeles (UPI) - The FBI has announced the discovery of the body of Nizar Gulam. He had been tortured and murdered. Mr. Gulam had been the subject of a massive police search following a tip that he might somehow be involved in the string of so-called "Boojum" Snark serial murders.

The grisly discovery followed an anonymous telephone tip to the hotline set up for seeking information from the public. The caller gave the body's location. The caller made no claim for any of the million-dollar reward that had been posted by the Justice Department.

The tip that led to Mr. Gulam's arrest warrant was provided by Rodney Bryer, owner of Catcher in the Rye Antiquarian Books in downtown L.A. Bryer had purchased some pages torn from an old edition of Lewis Carroll's notorious nonsense poem *The Hunting of the Snark* from Nizar Gulam, who claimed to have found them in a dumpster. Fingerprints on these pages led police to issue a warrant for Gulam's arrest.

Police remain puzzled why Gulam would have sold the pages rather than destroy them if he was the "Boojum" Snark serial killer. One theory is that he may have wanted to get caught, perhaps out of remorse for his crimes, or to stop him before he committed the next murder, unable to control the compulsion to do so himself.

The pages apparently have the names of the past victims written on them, as well as the names of what appear to be planned future victims. Police have refused to reveal who these future targets were.

The FBI and Nevada police have opened a homicide investigation into Nizar Gulam's murder.

Whoever killed Gulam methodically removed all traces of their footprints and tire tracks from the scene of the murder.

Casts have been taken from thirty different tire treads on the adjacent dirt road. Most have been identified as belonging to various ranch vehicles in the area.

Why Gulam was tortured also remains a mystery. The index fingers on both of his hands had been broken,

The lengthy article continued with a description of the past murders and attack attributed the "Boojum" Snark, as well as a photograph of Nizar Gulam. It was the same face in the Polaroid photo that Swat had given her and Babs breathed a sigh of relief. But what Babs didn't realize was that the fingerprints that were obvious on the image were not Swat's, but those of a random drunk that Swat had found passed out in an alley. It had been simple enough to press the unconscious man's hand on the photo.

At 9:00 a.m. sharp the doorbell rang. Babs went to the door carrying the suitcase that contained the other million dollars. She opened the door and handed him the case without saying anything, then closed the door. Swat returned to his car and counted the money.

Babs went immediately down to the basement and retrieved an explosive device she had made for use on one of the Carrollians and put it in the trunk of her car. That evening she made an excuse about going to a movie and went out, but made her way to Swat's office building instead. The building was open, as there was no money to pay for a receptionist or guard. She took the stairs to the tenth floor and broke into Swat's office. There was no alarm system since there was nothing in the office worth stealing. Inside she affixed the explosive to the underside of the swivel chair behind Swat's desk, along with a pressure sensitive trigger. She left, again by the stairs.

Babs was up again early the next morning to see if there had been a reported explosion, but there hadn't been. She had to wait for the evening edition for that bit of news.

RECEPTIONIST AT LOCAL P.I. FIRM KILLED IN EXPLOSION

Los Angeles (UPI) - Mary Anne Little, receptionist for a private investigation firm owned by former Rams lineman Pecheniuk 'Swat' Świątkiewicz, was killed today by a bomb placed under her employer's desk chair.

She was killed instantly by the powerful blast, evidently intended for Mr. Świątkiewicz.

No motive for the murder is known. However, it has been learned by UPI that Dr. Grant Kerr had recently employed Mr. Świątkiewicz as a bodyguard. Dr. Kerr, who is President of the California Chapter of the American Lewis Carroll Society, had apparently feared for his life because of the recent "Boojum" Snark murders.

Police had previously reported that the "Boojum Snark" murders had been solved with the discovery of the body of Nizar Gulam in the Nevada desert. LAPD spokesperson Nanoo Shepard told reporters today that they have reopened the case, and are focussing their attention on Rodney Breyer, owner of Catcher in the Rye Antiquarian Books.

Rodney Bryer provided the FBI with information that led police to issue an arrest warrant for Nizar Gulam. He has submitted a claim to the Justice Department for the one million dollar reward leading to the capture of the "Boojum" Snark serial killer.

Babs fought back the panic that tried to take her. She realized that Swat would be sure to seek revenge, if not for his secretary's death, then because he would realize that she had tried to kill him. "With my luck Mary Anne was probably his niece," Babs said aloud to herself. "What was she doing sitting in his damn chair?"

Babs went to the bank and retrieved the photo Swat had given her of Nizar Gulam's corpse. She bought a box of plain white envelopes, a BIC ballpoint pen and a ream of standard Xerox computer paper from an Office Depot, and took everything back home again. She went into her suite and put on latex gloves, then carefully wiped off any of her own fingerprints from around the edges and back of the Polaroid photo, using fingernail polish remover. Writing with her left hand to disguise her own handwriting, she addressed one of the envelopes to the FBI's Los Angeles branch office using the BIC ballpoint pen. She also wrote out a note that said simply: "GULAM KILLER PRINTS ON PHOTO." She folded the paper, put the note inside the envelope with the photo.

Having completed this task she gathered up the remaining paper, the ballpoint pen, the box of envelopes, and the book of postage stamps, and put them all in a plastic bag. She drove to the main post office in Hollywood and dropped the letter in an outside drop box. She then drove to a McDonald's restaurant and dumped the contents of the plastic bag into an outside trash can, then went inside to the Ladies Room, where she deposited the latex gloves in the paper towel waste bin.

She returned home and went back to her suite, where she got her pistol from her bedside table. After checking to be sure that it was loaded, she put the pistol in her purse. She packed a small suitcase, including a black jogging suit, a black ski mask, and black running shoes. She then went to the basement, where she retrieved two other explosive devices, some wire leads with alligator clips, a roll of duct tape, and a few simple hand tools, and put them all into a backpack. She drove out to the L. A. Airport and parked her Alpha Romeo in the long-term parking, then rented a midsize from Hertz.

She drove downtown, checked into the Marriott then drove over to Swat's office tower and parked on the roof of the parking structure across the street, where she could watch the building's entrance, to see if Swat would either show up or leave.

Three hours later she saw Swat enter the building. Babs got back in her car and exited, then parked on the street and waited twenty minutes until Swat left to get in his car, which he had parked on the street. She tailed his black Toyota, holding back a block or more so that he wouldn't get suspicious. They drove across town to a middleclass suburb in east L. A., pulled into the driveway of a small house and went inside. Babs drove by and noted the house number, then drove back to the Marriott.

After midnight she dressed in her black jogging suit and put the ski mask in her purse, then took the stairs down to the basement car parking level. She drove back out to Swat's neighbourhood and parked four blocks down the street from his house. She got the backpack with the bomb and tools out of the trunk and jogged casually along the quiet street. She ducked into Swat's driveway, then quickly slid under his Toyota. It took her only ten minutes to attach the bomb under the driver's seat and wire it to the ignition. Her task completed she slid back out from under the car and casually jogged back to her car, taking a roundabout route. She then drove back to the Marriott and went to bed.

The next morning she got out of bed when she heard room service slide the morning paper under her door. She opened and read the article on the bottom right of the front page.

FORMER RAM "SWAT" DIES IN EAST L. A. CAR BOMBING

Los Angeles (UPI) - Local Private Investigator and former Rams lineman Pecheniuk 'Swat' Świątkiewicz was killed this morning when a car bomb ripped through his automobile in his driveway.

The bomb set the car on fire and his body was burned beyond recognition. Police were able to identify the body through dental records, even though Świątkiewicz had lost most of his front teeth while playing football.

This morning's bombing falls on the heels of a failed attempt on his life yesterday at his office, in which his secretary, Mary Anne Little, was killed when she inadvertently triggered a bomb mounted under the seat of his desk chair.

Police are continuing to investigate whether Mr. Świątkiewicz and Ms. Little's deaths are related to the unsolved murder of Nizar Gulam, whom the police at one time believed to be "Boojum" Snark serial killer. Gulam's body was recently discovered in the Nevada desert. He had been tortured and died from a broken neck.

The article was continued on page two, giving a summary of the "Boojum" Snark killings, and a history of Swat's brief NFL football career. Babs threw the newspaper in the trashcan and went down for breakfast.

A few days later, when the FBI received Babs' letter with Gulam's photograph, they went into frantic action. The fingerprints were quickly identified as belonging to Yerani Dolash from LAPD records. He had been arrested innumerable times for drunkenness and vagrancy. A police search of the filthy streets and alleys of downtown L. A.'s tenderloin district had finally located his corpse inside a large cardboard box. His neck had been broken. Homicide opened a case, and the subsequent investigation revealed that Dolash had been in the LAPD drunk tank the night of Nizar Gulam's murder. His death was subsequently reported in the newspaper as a simple crime statistic, with no reference to any possible connection to the "Boojum" Snark murders.

A week after Swat's murder Grant Kerr received an envelope from an attorney, who said that he represented Mr. Świątkiewicz's estate. Inside was a numbered key to a footlocker at a private country club, along with the club's address. The letter said that Mr. Świątkiewicz's will had stipulated that he was to receive the key to this locker in the event of his death. Inside the locker there would be an envelope addressed to him. "Curiouser and curiouser!" Grant said aloud.

That evening Grant drove out to the country club and eventually located the locker. Inside he found, hidden beneath Swat's dirty golf clothes, a plain manila envelope with his name written across it. He removed the envelope, closed and locked the door, then dropped the key off at the member's counter. He went out to his car and opened the envelope. Inside was the other Polaroid of Nizar Gulam's corpse and a pocketsize cassette player/recorder. Grant thought he recognized Gulam's photo from mug shots he had seen in the newspapers. He pushed the play button on the cassette recorder and listened to the entire conversation between Babs and Swat. He rewound the tape and listened to it again two more times, before he believed what he had heard.

He sat in silence for the next twenty minutes, contemplating what he had heard.

He dropped the photograph and recorder back into the envelope and drove home. He went immediately to Babs' bedroom suite and opened the door without knocking. She was in bed, wearing a robe, reading a mystery novel.

"Didn't you ever hear of knocking?" she asked.

He ignored her. "I have something I'd like for you to hear."

"What? A new Lawrence Welk collection?"

He took the cassette recorder out, turned up the volume and pushed the play button. Babs' eyes went narrow as she listened.

"What have you got to say?" Grant demanded after it had played it through. He pulled out the photo that Swat had sent, along with the tape and held it up so she could see it.

She said nothing and just continued to stare coldly at him. "I'm calling the police," he said.

Babs reached under her pillow and produced her pistol, which she aimed at Grant's chest. "I don't think so. You're going to do exactly what 1 tell you to do or I'll kill you! Come on; we're going out onto the patio. Bring that stuff with you." She said this with such menace that Grant didn't resist, terrified at the gun pointing directly at him and realizing that he was confronted with a psychopathic killer. He hadn't imagined her being armed, and didn't even know that she owned a gun. She marched him outside to the grill.

"Take out the cassette and put it in that empty tin can, along with the photo," she demanded, pointing at a coffee can with the pistol. Grant fumbled with the recorder, but finally managed to get the cassette out, quite shaken by his predicament. "Now pour charcoal lighter in it." He fumbled with the plastic lid on the can. "I can never get these dang things open," he said. "Twist and lift! Twist and lift!" he thought. He finally succeeded, and soaked the cassette and Polaroid.

"Not set it alight!" she demanded.

"I don't have a match. You know I don't smoke."

"You're bloody hopeless!" she said.

"Where's a snark when you need one?" he thought.

She fished around in her robe pocket and produced a book of matches, which she tossed to him. He didn't manage to catch them, and had to bend over to pick them up.

"Clumsy idiot!" she said. He finally managed to set the contents aflame. "Now sit down on that chair." She motioned to a plastic lawn chair. Grant sat. They waited silently as the cassette and photo burned. Finally satisfied that the evidence was destroyed, she lowered the pistol. "I want a divorce," she said.

"I wouldn't think of contesting it."

"I'll be reasonable; I'll settle for sixty per cent of everything you have."

"Seems perfectly fair to me."

"You will have your book collection appraised and you can either pay me sixty per cent of the appraisal or have it auctioned and I will take sixty per cent of that. You can keep the house as long as you pay me sixty per cent of that appraisal as well. You'll move into a hotel until I find a place I like and move my things out. I want the Brancusi."

Grant nodded. "That will be fine. No problem."

"You have an hour to pack your bags and get out."

"I'll probably only need about twenty minutes; I'm a quick packer."

"Since when?"

Two months after their divorce was finalized Grant moved back into the Brentwood mansion. He was happy to be rid of Babs, even though she had exacted a very high financial price. He had been forced to re-mortgage the house. But he wouldn't really miss the money; he could always earn more than he knew what to do with in his lucrative profession. And best of all, he still had his precious books and the Dodgson photographs. He had auctioned all of the paintings at Sotheby's.

He had bought a sailboat, which he had named *The Boojum* as a sort of joke. He kept it moored down in Long Beach, and had become quite good at sailing it, even venturing out into the open Pacific when the winds weren't too strong.

The following February following his divorce he drove down to Long Beach for a cruise, and made his way to where *The Boojum* was docked. He went aboard and put his key in the lock to go into the small cabin below deck, only to find that it was already unlocked. He eased the door open and peered inside, half-expecting to see some beach bum asleep on his bunk. He was surprised to see instead a large black book. He went over to the bunk and picked it up, surprised to find that it was a copy of the Catalpa Press *Snark*. He opened it up and found to his dismay that some idiot had ripped out the entire first chapter, ruining the copy. There was a large bookmark inserted near the back, and he opened it to find that someone had drawn a large heart with a red pen next to the last stanza of the poem:

> *In the midst of the word he was trying to say,*
> *In the midst of his laughter and glee,*
> *He had softly and suddenly vanished away—*
> *For the Snark WAS a Boojum, you see.*

He dropped the book and rushed to get off of the boat. Babs, who was sitting on the deck of her powerboat tied up not far away, had been watching *The Boojum* intently through a pair of binoculars. She smiled as she saw the panic on George's face as he clambered back up onto the deck. When she pushed a button on the small transmitter she held in her hand the boat exploded in an enormous fireball. Acting the part of an innocent bystander, she screamed and dove to the deck of her boat.

After the debris had settled she eased herself up to look at what little remained. Boats on both sides of where *The Boojum* had been floating moments before were in flames. Thick black smoke billowed up from burning diesel and gasoline floating on the water.

"Happy Valentine, Grant," she said, and smiled that gorgeous smile of hers. She was wearing a pink leather micro-bikini for the occasion. Grant would have liked it.

᚜ᛚ ᚛ᛁᛚ ᛁᛈ Y ᚛ᛁᚱᛒᛁᚠ ᚛ ᛁ ᛁᚻᚻ Y ᚛ᛁ᚛ ᚛ᛁᛒ ᚛ᚱᚻᛁᛚ ᚛ᚻ᚛ᚱ,
Alice printed in the Ewellic Alphabet, 2013

Alis'z Advenčrz in Wundrland,
Alice printed in the Ñspel orthography, 2014

ˈ. ᒪ ᒷ ᒧ ˥ ᒧᒥ ˈ. ᒧ ˸ ˥ ᑌ ᒣ ˈˈ ᒧ ˥ ᒥ ᒷ ᑌ ᒷᑌ ᑌ ᒧ ˥ ᒧ ˞
ᒪ ˈ. ᑌ ᒧ, *Alice* printed in the Nyctographic Square Alphabet, 2011

·ᴊᴄɪꟅ'ɪꙅ ɹᒪꙅᴜᴸꙬᴐꙅ ɹɪ ·ʃᴜᴚ,ᴅᴄᴚᴜᒪ,
Alice printed in the Shaw Alphabet, 2013

ALISIZ ADVENCRZ IN WUNDRLAND,
Alice printed in the Unifon Alphabet, 2014

Behind the Looking-Glass: Reflections on the Myth of
Lewis Carroll, by Sherry L. Ackerman, 2012

Clara in Blunderland, by Caroline Lewis, 2010

Lost in Blunderland: The further adventures of Clara,
by Caroline Lewis, 2010

John Bull's Adventures in the Fiscal Wonderland,
by Charles Geake, 2010

The Westminster Alice, by H. H. Munro (Saki), 2010

Alice in Blunderland: An Iridescent Dream,
by John Kendrick Bangs, 2010

Rollo in Emblemland, by J. K. Bangs & C. R. Macauley, 2010

Gladys in Grammarland, by Audrey Mayhew Allen, 2010

Alice's Adventures in Pictureland,
by Florence Adèle Evans, 2011

Alices Hændelser i Vidunderlandet, *Alice* in Danish, 2015

La Aventuroj de Alicio en Mirlando,
Alice in Esperanto, by E. L. Kearney, 2009

La Aventuroj de Alico en Mirlando,
Alice in Esperanto, by Donald Broadribb, 2012

Trans la Spegulo kaj kion Alico trovis tie,
Looking-Glass in Esperanto, by Donald Broadribb, 2012

Les Aventures d'Alice au pays des merveilles,
Alice in French, 2010

Alice's Abenteuer im Wunderland, *Alice* in German, 2010

Alice's Adventirs in Wunnerlaun,
Alice in Glaswegian Scots, 2014

Nā Hana Kupanaha a ʻĀleka ma ka ʻĀina Kamahaʻo,
Alice in Hawaiian, 2012

Ma Loko o ke Aniani Kū a me ka Mea i Loaʻa iā ʻĀleka ma
Laila, *Looking-Glass* in Hawaiian, 2012

Aliz kalandjai Csodaországban, *Alice* in Hungarian, 2013

Eachtraí Eilíse i dTír na nIontas,
Alice in Irish, by Nicholas Williams, 2007

Lastall den Scáthán agus a bhFuair Eilís Ann Roimpi,
Looking-Glass in Irish, by Nicholas Williams, 2009

Eachtra Eibhlís i dTír na nIontas,
Alice in Irish, by Pádraig Ó Cadhla, 2014

Le Avventure di Alice nel Paese delle Meraviglie,
Alice in Italian, 2010

L's Aventuthes d'Alice en Êmèrvil'lie, *Alice* in Jèrriais, 2012

L'Travèrs du Mitheux et chein qu'Alice y dêmuchit,
Looking-Glass in Jèrriais, 2012

Las Aventuras de Alisia en el Paiz de las Maraviyas,
Alice in Ladino, 2014

Alisis pīdzeivuojumi Breinumu zemē, *Alice* in Latgalian, 2014

Alicia in Terra Mirabili, *Alice* in Latin, 2011

Alisa-ney Aventuras in Divalanda,
Alice in Lingua de Planeta (Lidepla), 2014

La aventuras de Alisia en la pais de mervelias,
Alice in Lingua Franca Nova, 2012

Alice ehr Eventüürn in 't Wunnerland,
Alice in Low German, 2010

Contoyrtyssyn Ealish ayns Çheer ny Yindyssyn,
Alice in Manx, 2010

Dee Erläwnisse von Alice em Wundalaund,
Alice in Mennonite Low German, 2012

The Aventures of Alys in Wondyr Lond,
Alice in Middle English, 2013

L'Aventuros de Alis in Marvoland, *Alice* in Neo, 2013

Ailice's Anters in Ferlielann, *Alice* in North-East Scots, 2012

Die Lissel ehr Erlebnisse im Wunnerland,
Alice in Palantine German, 2013

Соня въ царствѣ дива: Sonja in a Kingdom of Wonder,
Alice in Russian, 2013

Ia Aventures as Alice in Daumsenland,
Alice in Sambahsa, 2013

www.ingramcontent.com/pod-product-compliance
Lightning Source LLC
Chambersburg PA
CBHW030520260626
47157CB00005B/1817